THE BOARDING HOUSE

By

Guy Verreault

W & B Publishers
USA

W & B Publishers

For information:
W & B Publishers
Post Office Box 193
Colfax, NC 27235
www.a-argusbooks.com

ISBN: 9781942981145
ISBN: 1942981147

Book Cover designed by Dubya

Printed in the United States of America

Dedication

This is dedicated to the memory of Catherine Beaulieu – Verreault, my mother
Who had a boarding house of her own for many years!

CHAPTER ONE

(Late summer 1955)

" My dear Penelope," she read, "I hope you can find it in your heart to forgive. As you know I was always an easy mark for every con artist and stumblebum that came along; I guess I just got carried away with my own feelings of generosity. You will have to agree, though, that I always had good intentions. I think that I must have done some good along the way. I wish I could leave you millions of dollars, God knows you deserve it, for putting up with me all these years without the slightest adverse comment or complaint ever. There is a $10,000.00 sum of money that my attorney will turn over to you along with the deed to my mother's old Victorian house that I arranged to keep free and clear of any debts. I have to confess something to you; remember the times you picked up the tab when I was gone or too busy to do it? Well, most of those times I did it on purpose because I was broke, flat out of cash, too proud to tell you or borrow it from you under any kind of pretence. It nearly killed me the year I had to ask you to work without the guarantee of a salary because my cash was all tied up in one of my projects. I could never have told you this face

to face. Maybe my mother's old Victorian house will make up for some of the hardship I must have caused you. I guess the only thing left to say, my dearest Penelope, is good-bye, and try to keep a charitable thought for your bungling old boss."

Just a few weeks ago she and Jason McKee had been sunning themselves on the beaches of Havana in Cuba. Although Jason liked a glass of good wine, he was not a heavy drinker. Nothing in his behavior or appearance could have foretold a severe heart defect. He died in his sleep. When Penelope called him for breakfast that fateful Sunday morning, she was near tears and full of fear when Jason did not respond to her calls. She had never even cried over her loss. The long plane ride to Calgary, Alberta had not given her time to sort out her thoughts. She had been too busy making arrangements to have Jason's remains shipped back to Canada to arrange a funeral. He had many friends but no living relatives, everything had been left to her.

She had doubted that her inheritance would amount to much. Jason was a notorious soft touch to people with "off the wall" projects. Penelope was afraid that most of his money had been spent on what he would pleasantly refer to as his "pet projects" == like the time he financed the comeback of his favorite female star in a new motion picture. That project, as she recalled, totally failed. After spending several thousand dollars of Jason's money on her third face-lift, the star was just 'too far-gone to come back.'

The day had started unpleasantly. Things had moved so swiftly in the past few days that she felt like a sleepwalker. She got off the plane, went into the terminal, picked up her luggage then walked to the taxi stand just outside the main doors. She handed her suitcase to the driver before settling herself in the back seat. Since it was still mid-morning she asked the driver to take her to downtown Victoria where she was to meet with Julian H. Brennington, the senior partner in the law firm that handled her former boss's estate and affairs.

Mr. Brennington had made the arrangements for Penelope to fly from Calgary to Victoria. She was on her way to his office to get a copy of Jason's will.

The taxi finally drew up in front of the massive imposing gray building, the offices of Brennington & Associates. Penelope stepped out of the taxi and paid her fare. Clutching her hand luggage, she stood silently on the curb for several minutes, unwilling to face the ordeal she was sure awaited her. The fact that she was a natural worrier did not help her peace of mind. Earlier in the week, when she had spoken with the lawyer on the telephone, he had informed her that she was Jason McKee's only heir. He'd never married, had no siblings, his mother had passed away a few years ago.

Penelope finally forced herself to climb the three steps leading to the front door of the building and reluctantly walked in. Julian Brennington greeted her at the massive oak door of his inner office. He was a tall, good-looking individual with an air of arrogance. In a matter of fact manner he asked her to take a seat. It was obvious to Penelope that there would be no small talk with this man.

"Miss Woodspring," he said in a somber voice, "I am sorry to say that what I'm about to disclose to you may not be the most pleasing news you would have liked to hear. It is a very sad commentary that an intelligent man such as Jason McKee wasted a rather large sum of money, one might even say a fortune, on an array of misfits including inappropriate projects that certainly did not deserve his generosity". As he handed her an envelope he said, "Here's a letter that Mr. McKee left for you."

She immediately opened the envelope and began reading the letter.

Penelope wiped a stray tear away from her cheek and settled heavily back into the overstuffed red leather chair.

At thirty-six, Penelope had been his secretary for over fifteen years. Everyone knew that she was more than just a secretary, but no one dared to insinuate they were lovers. Jason was a free-lance reporter for several newspaper chains. His assignments had sent them globetrotting several times a year. In one stroke his sudden death had not only taken her lifetime companion but had robbed her of a career she enjoyed tremendously.

Brennington went to his desk drawer to retrieve two envelopes. He opened the first one, and handed her a check asking her to sign the release attached to it. She kept the check then gave him back the release for his files. She noticed the amount of money on the check was not the full ten thousand dollars mentioned in Jason's letter. As she raised her eyebrows, the lawyer quickly mentioned he had deducted the amount of the plane fare from Calgary to Victoria. She placed the check in her purse as he handed her the second envelope with the deed to an old house on Victoria's Military Street.   Penelope didn't have a clue how to get there but was in no mood to inquire from Brennington.

The lawyer told her the house was a rather large dwelling on almost two acres of land. It was somewhat in need of repairs. He added that she might want to sell it.

Hans Kriegel, a real estate broker who would give her the keys, might be the right person to help. He handed her Kriegel's business card. Tact in these circumstances was certainly not Brennington's strongest point. Penelope thought that in dealing with sensitive situations, this lawyer had the finesse of a charging rhino. Especially with strong-willed women, he appeared to be ill at ease.

Striving to hide her disappointment, Penelope asked the lawyer how fifteen plus years as a roving secretary as well as companion prepared one to be the mistress of an eighty-year-old mansion. In opening the envelope containing the deed to the house she glanced at the street number given on the papers. *I just hope that number 13 isn't some kind of an omen!* But she felt somewhat relieved to find an attached receipt showing that all property, school and other taxes were paid for the coming year.

The lawyer watched her read the receipt, mentioning she should make sure to keep those papers in a safe place. He then added, "By the way, how exactly did Jason McKee die? I was never made aware of any of the details surrounding his death. All I know is that he was killed somewhere in Cuba while doing some investigative reporting on the American gambling casinos and their owners."

"Well," she said, "you're never going to believe this. After thirty years of travelling all over the world, slogging through the most dangerous jungles, covering front line action in three wars, poor Mr. McKee was killed by a coconut thrown at him by a vindictive monkey that he was trying to photograph."

Brennington's face showed only blank surprise. She did not know whether he believed her or not, but as she was leaving the office, Penelope could have sworn she heard him chuckling to himself. *Oh well,* she thought, *what could you expect but a morbid sense of humor from an old vulture like him?*

In the reception area she called Hans Kriegel, the real-estate broker in charge of safekeeping Mrs. McKee's property. He sounded like an accommodating person on the telephone. Kriegel agreed to meet Penelope at his office within the half-hour.

She was pleased he could show her the property on such short notice. But as she waited for a taxi, she couldn't help wondering if the day held further unpleasant surprises. What was so mysterious about Mrs. McKee's old house?

***

Kriegel was a tall man with reddish-blond hair and a permanent smile on his face. He greeted Penelope politely but was in the middle of closing a "big deal." Would she mind going to have a first look at the property by herself? Then let him know what she wanted to do with the old mansion? For instance he said, would she want to live in it for a time or place it on the market immediately?

Penelope agreed to have a quick look at the Victorian house. However, she had to catch a return flight to Calgary in the next three hours. She would call him from home after deciding what to do.

***

When she arrived at 13 Military Street she was somewhat disappointed. It appeared to be worse that she could have imagined. As she pushed open the gate it swung off one hinge to lodge against a clump of weed growing through the cracked cement sidewalk. One of the wide steps leading to the front door was badly damaged; the windows had not been washed for some time. It was a huge three-story structure with extensive architectural details that only the late 19th century could bring. The house had received a recent coat of paint that gave the whole place a clean look. The front verandah was huge in comparison with other neighborhood houses. A quick look on the outside was all she wanted. She had had enough surprises for the day. She noticed that there was a smaller building at the rear of the mansion, wondering if they belonged together. She liked what she saw but realized some work would have to be done. How much work? That would have to be determined once her mind was set on whether she kept the house or sold it.

***

The return flight was without incident, just a long wait. Penelope had time to think through the events of the past few hours. She had some savings plus the almost $10,000 check from the lawyer. Her first thought was to sell the property but that meant she would have to be in Victoria for an undetermined period of time. The thought of returning to Victoria alone plus having to deal with total strangers didn't appeal to her. She would wait until she got home, let everything turn over in her mind again then decide on a plan of action.

The first thing she did when she arrived home was to call Hans Kriegel as she had promised. He was, if anything, less encouraging than Brennington had been about the likelihood of a quick sale on the old property.

"Well, I don't know, Miss Woodspring, white elephants are always hard to sell quickly. It's just the way the economy is right now. House sales here in Victoria are down, consequently so are prices. In the shape it's in, it could take months or even a year to sell. I'm not willing to touch it until some repairs are done."

That's that! thought Penelope, as she hung up. The thing to do was to pack up, and move to Victoria to do something with the old mansion. She'd live in it for a time, fix it up just enough to attract a prospective buyer. Perhaps then Kriegel would think more positively. Would she be undertaking too much? She called her brother Sam, her only relative, the person she trusted most.

Sam was a fairly good carpenter who could be very helpful. Besides, something had to happen before she ran out of ready cash.

Sam agreed to come to dinner with her so that she could tell him about her visit to Victoria. Dinner with his younger sister was just what Sam needed for a change.

***

When her brother arrived, Penelope was all excited about telling him what she had in mind. She described as best she could the condition of the exterior of the house, which was all she had seen.

Would he like to move to Victoria to help her get this inheritance in a good enough state of repairs in order to sell it fast? This move would only be temporary she said to Sam, but in her subconscious something told her that it would not be the case. Was she making a good or bad move? Time alone would tell if her choice had been right.

Without a moment of hesitation Sam agreed to his sister's suggestion and asked her when she would like to make the move.

"How about tomorrow Sam," she said. "The sooner the better, don't you think? If you agree I'll make the reservations immediately. I'm going to take the early flight; you can join me later in the day."

"It's okay with me, Penelope," Sam answered. "Tomorrow will be fine; I look forward to the move. Victoria is a nice place to visit this time of year. Let's have a look at this old house. Then I can see how much work needs to be done."

Penelope picked up the telephone, called the airline to make the reservations for the two of them. As she hung up the phone Sam told his sister that he better get to his place to pack his suitcase for tomorrow's trip. When he left, he turned towards his sister showing a grin on his face and said, "See you tomorrow in Victoria, Sis."

While Penelope was preparing for her adventure to Victoria, she thought, *I suppose that I may never know which of these will be the bigger mistake, going to Victoria or getting my brother Sam to join me.* Her brother was forty-six, not a Valentino, but extremely likable. The most charitable description would be "A charmer."

***

When she awoke the next morning, she thought about how easy it had been to convince her brother to join her in Victoria. It made her wonder if she was doing the right thing by moving to Victoria. Was this a warning of things to come? She pushed the thoughts out of her mind, called for a taxi to take her to the airport for her flight to an unknown adventure in Victoria, British Columbia.

***

As her plane touched down in Victoria in early afternoon she became anxious. The dream was still with her. It hadn't exactly been unpleasant, yet... as she wheeled her luggage cart from the terminal into the blazing sun, she couldn't help shivering.

CHAPTER TWO

"13 Military Street" the cab driver repeated Penelope's destination as they pulled out of the taxi stand. "You know that sounds familiar to me. If I'm not mistaken, this used to be old Mrs. McKee's house! Are you a relative?" But before she could answer the driver went on to say the place had been vacant for some time.

"There are rumors going around," he said, "that the house is haunted. They say Mrs. McKee died under suspicious circumstances, but nothing ever came out of it. That was about two years ago. Did you say you were related?"

"Not at all," replied Penelope. "I now own the property. My boss of over fifteen years was Mrs. McKee's son, Jason. When he passed away last winter, I found out that he had willed the property to me. I was here a few days ago, fell in love with all of Victoria but especially with the old Victorian house on Military Street. I saw that it has a lot of potential. Furthermore, my brother Sam being a good carpenter as well as a good handyman has agreed to come live with me for a while to fix what has to be fixed."

When they arrived at her destination, Penelope asked the driver if he would be kind enough to bring her bags inside the house. She walked up the four steps, went to the mail box to find extra keys as Kriegel said there would be. She opened the front door holding it back for the cab driver to bring her heavy suitcases in. She paid him handsomely took his card, as she might need to hire his services in the near future. *Jack Storm,* the card read, including his telephone numbers.

She touched a light switch on the wall to find the electricity had been turned on. Obviously Mr. Kriegel was performing his real-estate duties in a very efficient manner. Everything appeared to be freshly cleaned as she noticed for the first time that the entranceway was a very large room with a marble floor. A crystal chandelier hung from the center of the ceiling. To the left were some closets or wardrobes that must have been used at one time to hold the guests' coats. Looking at her luggage, which Jack Storm had placed against the wall, the thought came to her that many of the people who once came to this house probably never walked further than this point. If she knew anything about Victorian butlers from her readings, this was one of their duties; stop the people from walking in further until he knew if they were wanted.

Penelope opened one of her suitcases. She needed to find a warm sweater or jacket, as the house was cool.

***

The time must have gone by faster than she thought, as suddenly she heard a thud in addition to a moan. Like someone falling on the stairs which made her realize that Sam had arrived.

He burst into the large room giving her his usual bear hug. "Say, Sis," he enthused, "I think this whole idea of moving here is the greatest. Do you realize that Victoria is a place chock full of old money? Why in no time at all we'll have this place sold."

Obviously, he has never heard of 'white elephants', thought Penelope, as Sam rambled on. "How many rooms does it have?" "

I don't really know, Sam," she managed to squeeze in before he forged ahead hardly pausing for breath.

"Maybe the property is large enough to sub-divide; or maybe we could convert it into a hotel. Of course it will need some fixing up. But I can take care of that," he said.

"Yes," she replied warily, "we can do all these things." It was not that Penelope was bitter or cynical, but after all she'd had fifteen years of Jason's projects to prepare for the worst. All she could envision at this point was the house lying in ruins while potential buyers or (if the house was converted into a hotel) guests running for the nearest shelter to avoid falling timbers as well as gushing pipes. Penelope looked down the hall thankful to see that the telephone was hooked up, just as Hans Kriegel had promised.

"The first thing we must do, Sam, is buy some groceries for ourselves. Let me call the taxi driver who drove me here from the airport."

***

Jack Storm was there promptly. Just after leaving the grocery store, they wheeled up Military Street, past many of the houses known by some euphemistically as mid-Victorian.

"Grandmother called them 'gingerbread houses,' Father on the other hand, called them junky," Penelope said. "These homes were built in an era when a dollar was worth a dollar."

The people who had a million of those dollars were few and far between. The houses were constructed on the theory that the more "gingerbread" they were adorned with, the more affluent was the owner. According to this theory, the builder of Penelope's house must have been the richest man in town. The sight that greeted their startled eyes would surely have given pause to even the most ardent devotees of Victorian architecture.

Number 13 Military Street was a huge three-story structure painted a virgin white, sprouting ornate towers from all four corners. Every available eave, ell and rain gutter boasted scrolls, frills as well as fretwork that made the whole thing look like a tremendous pile of Grandma's lace collars.

Each side of the green lawn was about the size of an Olympic swimming pool. The long curving white gravel drive was almost half a city block in length. Then there was a white marble fountain complete with a fully clothed statue of Diana the huntress, in the center of the lawn. The effect of the place from the outside with the sun shining on it was overwhelming, even to Penelope who had seen all kinds of architecture in her globe-trotting days.

"Boy, that's what I call a house," Sam said.

"Looks more like a birthday cake to me," said Penelope with something less than wild and uncontrollable joy. "We've seen the entrance hall, now let's go in to admire the rest of this old mansion and pray that all is fine or at least close to being fine."

They ascended the broad steps onto a porch half the size of Penelope's former apartment in Calgary. Suddenly she felt like a real intruder, the huge stained glass windows staring ominously at her; their many tiny panes strongly resembling pictures she had seen of greatly magnified eyes of insects. They entered the large marbled-floor room with its enormous chandelier and walked through to the end of the hall.

With more bravado than they felt, they threw open the two solid oak doors that faced them, entering a long hall running the entire length of the house. They could see at a glance that the exterior of the house had been kept up merely as a façade to fool the nosy neighbors. The floors, though they appeared to be of the best quality parquet, were mostly bare of varnish in addition to being quite rough. The huge crystal chandelier must have been a thing of beauty at one time, but was now missing many of its crystals. It hung at a crazy angle. To the left was what used to be known in the old days as a parlor.

It was at least thirty feet long, twenty-five wide, furnished with that type of furniture most favored by the Victorian era. You know, the kind that was as uncomfortable and as ugly as human ingenuity could make it. The pieces that were not covered with faded red velvet were covered with slippery frayed horsehair. The whole room was dominated by the most gigantic upright piano they had ever seen. It was so ornately carved that a pin could not have been placed on it without puncturing the eyeball of a cupid or a dove.

Behind the parlor was what used to be called a library, which was certainly a misnomer since it contained not a single book. It held about ten huge leather chairs. As they would later discover, they were the only comfortable ones anywhere in the house. This, perhaps, was due to the fact that Victorian men spent most of their time in the library, and like most men of that era, they were not as willing to sacrifice comfort for style as their wives were. The walls were lined with a collection of animal heads.

"How anyone could relax with the beady eyes of a rhino staring at him is beyond me, but I gave up probing the male mind at the age of nine," commented Penelope.

At the end of the hall were the maid's quarters. This was a truly Spartan room containing a single bed, chest of drawers and a chamber pot. This last item quickly drew Penelope's immediate attention. She wondered wildly if it were a portent of things to come. Ardently wishing she had been a better history student, she struggled vainly to recall whether or not they had indoor plumbing in the Victorian era. The next room, the kitchen, did not calm her fears. There were two old fashion spigots in the sink, which when turned on, gushed rusty cold water and rustier lukewarm water from the hot spigot. The stove was one of those old style wood-coal-burning monsters her grandmother used to slave over for hours on end. They entered the dining room, which was really the only saving grace of the whole lower floor. This magnificent room contained a Honduras mahogany table with hardly any carving except on the legs. Fourteen graceful Queen Anne chairs surrounded it. An elegant Georgian buffet filled an entire wall, together with a huge crystal chandelier hanging over the table. It was in excellent repair. The floor was carpeted with a genuine Oriental rug, which could have brought six to ten thousand dollars at any antique auction. Some thoughtful soul had left the service room, to the rear of the dining room, filled with a multitude of gold-plated china, gold flatware as well as cut glass crystal.

"We can at least eat our TV-dinners in style," said Sam. "What a place," he added. "I'm going to have my tools sent here from Calgary. I can see there are a lot of repairs to be done. It will certainly take several months to put this wonderful house in decent condition." Penelope was happy that Sam was in a cheerful fixing mood.

***

Their first night in the old mansion was, to say the least, quite eventful. Kriegel had told

Penelope the utilities had been turned on, but had not given her a map or blueprint to the location of wall plugs or gas pipes. They spent hours crawling around on all fours searching for a place to plug in a lamp or hook-up the only gas heater they had found in one of the bathrooms.

Oh! Yes, about those bathrooms, Victorian houses do have indoor plumbing. Each floor had two bathrooms containing a free-standing washbasin, an old fashioned bath-tub perched on four claw feet in the shape of lion's paws that looked like they would attack the bather at any time.

After quickly visiting the second floor, Penelope and Sam went up one more flight of stairs. To their amazement they found every room furnished properly. In the bathrooms they found a water closet with the tank perched high on the wall. From the tank hung a long chain which, when pulled would release cascades of water that often as not would be more than sufficient to flush the toilet.

On cold mornings these tanks would "sweat" large drops of water that would drip down the neck of the one using the facility. Getting back to the utility problem, the only working wall plug they could find was in the parlor. By some stroke of luck the gasman had done a thorough inspection of all gas jets and outlets. He must've found them to be working well.

***

The brother and sister team ate their take-out Chinese dinner by candlelight then retreated to

the library for seating comfort. Penelope had decided the daylight of the next day would be much
better to inspect the rest of the house. She certainly didn't want any surprises in the dark. The day
had been long enough and tiresome at that, the
tension of the unknown making her edgy.

She decided that they should sleep in the
parlor since there were two wonderful heavily
stuffed davenports.

Sam objected immediately to this arrangement. He didn't like, at his age, sleeping in
the same room where his sister was sleeping herself.

When going to bed Penelope wore a long
flannel nightgown, a nightcap and long woolen
socks. She could hardly see the logic in her brother's modesty. She doubted seriously that even
cloistered nuns went to bed with more clothing
than she did. To avoid a long futile argument she
decided to stay the night in the maid's quarters
where she would not have to put up with her own
brother's foibles.

***

The next morning Penelope awoke stiff as
a board and cold as a miser's heart. Victoria's late
summer nights can be very humid and chill your
bones if you are not acclimatized. She dragged
herself out of bed, went to the kitchen to do battle
with Count Dracula, the new name given to the
ancient kitchen stove. By the time she had an ade-
quate fire going, Sam came bouncing into the

kitchen with that early morning cheerfulness that she had always abhorred.

"Well! My dear sister," Sam said, "the first thing we have to do is buy a car to get around in this burg, then we can start fixing this old mausoleum a bit."

Now Sam may have been bumbling, but what he lacked in manual dexterity he more than made up for in fox-like cunning. He knew very well that Penelope was not worth a tinker's damn before noon. He had just chosen the best possible time to spring the idea of a car on his sister. At nine o'clock in the morning, Penelope would have agreed to buy a brand new Cadillac to avoid an argument.

"Well, I guess you're right," she said lazily, "but we'll have to find something rather inexpensive as I don't intend to spend too much money on transportation."

As to his suggestion of fixing up the house, she refused even to discuss it immediately. She had had plenty of experience in her time redecorating rundown places, but nothing that would prepare her for attacking a fifteen-room Victorian mansion badly in need of a face lift from bottom to top. She was conscious that Sam could be a great help, as long as she kept an eye on him. But, he could also be a hindrance if left on his own too long.

After a full country-style breakfast with a good cup of coffee, they decided to set off on foot in the general direction of downtown Victoria.

It wasn't long before they saw what looked like a parking lot with different makes of automobiles. There was a crude small building at the rear of it with a sign that said:

"We buy, sell or trade. Transportation for every pocket book!

Open six days a week!"

"There it is!" said Sam. "Just what we've been looking for."

"Yes, I'm sure it is," said Penelope.

As soon as they reached the place, Sam barged right in, started busily kicking tires and slamming doors, in that insane way that most males have of displaying their inbred knowledge of cars!

Penelope just stood there looking for a place to sit down. A man in his forties walked towards her from the far end of the lot. He was dressed in a cheap brown suit, red flannel tie and brown shoes buffed to a dazzling shine. His hair was slicked back close to his head. He had the most perfect shining white teeth she had ever seen on anything outside of a sperm whale!

"Can I help you today?" the man asked with an ingratiating smile.

"Why yes," she said, "I'm looking for a cheap car!"

"Madam," he said in a voice that registered hurt, shame and indignation all at once, "we don't sell cheap cars here. However, we do have some real bargains on low-mileage older automobiles that have hardly been used. Like this Danton here who was only driven by one owner to attend church on Sunday. It's obviously a steal at $1995.00!"

"Well I don't know," Penelope was saying as Sam came trotting up next to her.

"Say, that buggy has real class," he blurted out, but did not say any more as he was too busy rubbing his shins where his sister had given him a swift kick.

"I think that we need something a little smaller, more economical in fuel consumption," she said studiously avoiding the word 'cheap.'

"I have just what you've got in mind. Kindly follow me please!" said the salesman.

He took them to the back of the lot where stood a whole row of real "refugees." Nestled among these however, was a car that immediately caught Penelope's eye. It strongly resembled a large green beetle whose round glass eyes stared at her soulfully. She had always felt a soft touch for the underdog. Besides, she was sure that no one but her would be fool enough to buy this poor thing. Trying to appear nonchalant she said, "How much is that green one?"

Sensing a sale, the salesman perked up and said, "Oh, that's one of those Volkswagens, they're hot sellers you know."

"How can that be?" Penelope replied. "It looks as if it's been sitting there for some time. Besides," she added, "it has a hole in the roof."

"They call that a sunroof," the salesman replied in a superior male tone. "It makes the car look like a convertible. Tell you what, I'll throw in a full tank of gas and sell it to you for $550.00! Do we have a deal?"

To Penelope this sounded like a real bargain. She was so tired she would almost have been willing to pay that much just to sit in a car.

When she finally wrote out a check, received the papers to the car and started to get in, Sam began to protest. She ordered him to the front seat on the passenger side. It had been more years than she cared to remember since Penelope had driven what Sam referred to as a "stick shift." Once she properly recalled the intricacies of clutch, gas pedal along with gear positions, the car buzzed happily along. It seemed to be quite grateful that someone had taken pity on it!

"See, beauty is only skin deep!" it seemed to say.

Sam immediately nicknamed it, 'Agnes,' after a girl friend he had in high school that he said, was just about as ugly as well as being the same shape as the car.

"Oh well," he remarked gloomily, "at least I'm a good enough mechanic to keep this buggy running."

Penelope knew he was speaking the truth. Her brother had owned a series of old wrecks, which he somehow had managed to keep on the road where anyone else would have consigned them to the junkyard.

Since his accident three and a half years earlier, Sam at times was not in full control of his abilities, having had a serious fall at a construction project that landed him in the hospital for several months. Sam had been placed on permanent disability because of his inability to concentrate for long periods of time.

Now that the car problem was settled, Penelope decided it was urgent to tackle the redecorating of the old mansion. Sam as usual oversimplified everything. He seemed to think that the whole process would consist of slapping on a few coats of paint, tearing-out a partition or two in addition to rearranging some furniture!

Penelope knew better. The thought of the unknown made her a bit uncomfortable. What did she get herself into, she kept thinking!

CHAPTER THREE...

Early one sunny morning Penelope was cutting roses from her front bushes when a voice coming from the sidewalk startled her. As she turned around to see who it was as well as what the person wanted, she was struck with a vision from the past. Here was a man about six feet tall, in his early fifties, fairly well-dressed who strangely resembled her late benefactor. *My God,* she thought, *he looks just like Jason!* It just stunned her for a moment. When she recovered she said "Goodmorning sir, what can I do for you?"

"I was just admiring the architecture of your beautiful house. It stands out on its own in this neighborhood. This is my second visit to Victoria, I plan to set up a local import/export business soon. By the way, I'm Richard Taylor. I sure wish I could live in an area like this one. Would you know of anyone having a room or suite for rent?"

Penelope was bothered by this man's re-semblance to Jason McKee. He could have been his twin brother. "I'm Penelope Woodspring," she said. "I own this old house which I intend to turn into a boarding house soon. When do you need this place?" she asked.

"Possibly on my next trip in three to four weeks, Mrs. Woodspring. At this moment I'm negotiating the purchase of a piece of land near the water, in order to build the warehouse I'll need for my import business."

Penelope told him she was going to have to make a decision in the next few days concerning this old house. "Why don't you call me on your return trip, by then I'll know for certain if I'll be taking on boarders. Here's my telephone number."

"That sounds fantastic to me, Mrs. Woodspring, I'm glad I walked by here this morning. You'll hear from me soon," said Richard as he left Penelope standing there in some kind of a trance.

Seeing Richard Taylor with his close physical resemblance to McKee brought back some pleasant memories as well as tears at the same time. Jason's death was still fresh in her mind. Penelope could not have foreseen the danger ahead. She hurried the cutting of the roses and walked back into her house to a world of reality.

Repairs and renovations were on her mind but the first problem to avoid, as always, would be overspending. After having had a good look through the house, Penelope felt that there seemed to be too much furniture just sitting there. She decided to take "Agnes" on a drive to the library to look for a listing of antique dealers in Victoria. She only wanted to sell a few pieces to make the rooms a bit more spacious.

The parlor certainly had a davenport and chair too many. Other rooms also needed thinning out, without too much depleting that is.

At the library she found a book which listed local reputable antique dealers. While talking with one of the librarians she got the name of John Smyth who was recommended as one you could trust.

When Penelope got home, she called Mr. Smyth, who showed avid interest at being recommended by the local librarian. He informed her that he would be at her place in about two hours. In the meantime, she decided to go through the rooms again to have a better mental picture of which pieces she would want to sell immediately. By the time John Smyth left with a pick-up truckload of furniture, Miss Woodspring had a check in her hands in the amount of $8,500.00, not to mention a pleased feeling at having been a very astute businesswoman.

She suddenly remembered the dream she had had prior to leaving Calgary. "A Boarding House," she said aloud as her brother Sam walked in!

"What a fantastic idea," he said. "I can certainly get a sign ready and we're in business!"

"Not so fast, dear brother, I was just thinking out loud. It was only a dream I had the night before leaving Calgary to come to Victoria. We should talk about it. If it can be done, look into the possibility of making it happen! There would be a lot of cleaning-up, painting, wallpapering etc., before it can become reality. Let's sleep on this and come back to it with a clear mind in the morning, if you don't mind?" *I may even have a boarder already,* she thought to herself remembering the gentleman who had spoken to her from the sidewalk.

***

The next day Sam and Penelope had a council of war on redecorating the house. She had to reject some of Sam's more grandiose ideas like Italian marble sunken tubs in every bathroom and wall-to-wall carpeting in every bedroom. They finally got down to the essentials. She realized they would have to rewire a major portion if not the whole house, and definitely install a few more gas outlets to compensate for not having a central heating system. They also knew that the majority of the bathrooms (9 in all), would have to be updated if used on a daily basis. They made a list of what had to be done urgently including refinishing some of the beautiful hardwood floors.

She had redecorated many small apartments in the past but a project this size was somewhat scary! Paint, wallpaper and all the needed accessories would require several trips to the store.

When she returned home, Sam was there eager to get started. His tools had arrived by bus from Calgary. He needed the car to go down to the bus depot to get them.

***

The following day they got their act together, put on old clothes to begin the tedious job
of painting this old mansion. It had to be made
presentable to possible "boarders."

Penelope had been painting steadily for
several hours when she began to get a very uneasy
feeling in the pit of her stomach. It was a strange
queasy feeling she could not quite put her finger
on yet, could not shake it off either! It suddenly hit
her! She knew exactly what it was.

Considering the crashes and yells that
were always part of any project where Sam was
involved in, she felt she should have been able to
hear him from upstairs even through the thick
floors of the old mansion.

Quite the contrary, there was dead silence
when she stopped working to listen!

*Either he's goofing off down there, or he's
botched something up,* she thought. "In any case,
I'd better go down to check on him," she mur-
mured aloud.

Penelope placed her brush on the paint
can she was using then ran to the library where
Sam had been painting. As she entered the room,
she was surprised to see that three neatly painted
walls were completed but, no sign of Sam! I wonder where he could be, she thought.

A paint can was lying on its side with
some paint spilled onto the floor near the wall
lined with empty bookshelves. He probably
tripped over the can and ran off somewhere to escape my wrath, as well he might, she thought to
herself.

She walked over to the tilted can, set it upright, then walked into the kitchen to get some paint thinner along with extra rags to clean up the mess, not particularly happy to do so. Penelope was more aggravated by the fact that Sam was nowhere in sight! She started to look for her brother in different downstairs locations, even outside around the back of the house, but Sam was not answering her calls. She went back to the library. She was angrily looking around the room when she suddenly heard faint cries and muffled pounding coming from the unpainted wall. Penelope walked towards the "bookless" shelves, put an ear to the wall. She heard Sam's voice coming from a distance as if he were in a well or very hollow chamber!

"Sam!" she cried. "Where are you?"

"I'm behind this blankety-blank wall," replied this faint voice.

"Well!" she exclaimed; "how in the world did you get in there?"

"I don't know," Sam shouted. "I was painting along like crazy when all of a sudden as I leaned backwards, the whole wall caved in, and I with it!

"I don't know how I'm going to get you out of there if you can't remember how you got yourself in there in the first place."

"Call the fire department or something," he yelled! "It's hot in here. Besides, the paint is drying fast."

"What paint! Don't tell me that you're wasting paint on the inside of the walls."

"Of course not," Sam immediately replied. "I meant the paint that I spilled on myself," he said.

"Oh, no!" she gasped, leaning her head wearily against the wall. In a flash the wall gave way with a bang. Penelope fell full length on Sam who was covered with white paint. They struggled a bit and managed to get to their feet. As she stepped backwards, the half-dried paint from Sam's shirt stuck to Penelope's dress and stained it.

"Well Sam," she said angrily, "I should have known that if there were one secret panel in this house you would find it at the exact moment you had a full bucket of paint in your hands!"

She pushed the wall on the opposite side making it open to allow them to return on the library side.

Both of them spent the rest of the day cleaning the mess from the floor where Sam had spilled the paint.

***

The following morning when Penelope walked into the library, she realized that Sam had almost finished the needed work. She was able to complete the job in less than three hours. She then proceeded to the maid's quarters. She was working along diligently when the wall in front of her suddenly gave way. She was fortunate enough not to fall forward as she had done the previous day in the library.

The panel stayed a little ajar so Penelope decided to do some exploring. She placed her full can of paint to prevent the panel from shutting on her. She then stepped into what can be described as a narrow dark passageway draped with cobwebs. The passageway was rather short, it led behind the bathroom and under the back stairs to the library. Suddenly Penelope's quick mind began to hum like a well-tuned engine. *Library equals master of the house, plus maid's quarters, equals hanky-panky,* she thought. How interesting it was becoming to find this secret passageway! She could imagine a jaded old man as he told his wife goodnight, went into the library, pressed the secret panel and slunk down the passageway to a midnight rendezvous with the young beautiful maid. *Well,* she thought, *Victorians were not so simon-pure after all!*

She had always felt that sin was not an original invention of the younger generation, now she had positive proof. She mustn't tell Sam about the passageway to the maid's quarters. It's not that she didn't trust her own brother, she just did not believe in placing temptation in the way of the feeble male libido!

The painting was progressing steadily, but the size of the project was gigantic and Penelope could see that they were going to spend the rest of their lives doing redecorating if she didn't get some extra help.

It was at this point that Edward showed up.

***

One morning while sitting at the kitchen table sipping her cup of coffee looking ruefully at her work-gnarled hands, she heard a timid knock at the back door. She walked over to the door, opened it just wide enough to get a glimpse of a little old man with a face that had been exposed to the sun a bit too long!

"Good morning madam," the man said in a bit of a drawl. "My name is Edward Stone. I'm the handyman in the neighborhood. I've been around for some time, just about thirty years. Would you have any small chores that need to be done?"

Penelope certainly did have some "little chores" that very urgently needed to be done. But, from the looks of Edward, about the heaviest work he appeared to be cut out for would be pruning the roses and watering the lawn!

How wrong can a snap judgment be? She would soon find out. In this age of specialization, Edward was one of those rare jewels, a "Jack-of-all-trades". Once he was informed what they were doing, more importantly what needed to be done, he took over the whole operation.

His frail body concealed a human dynamo of energy. He knew how to do wiring, was an excellent plumber as well as a good carpenter. Best of all he knew exactly how to get the most work out of her brother Sam, with the least possible disasters. Mostly, he just delegated the more simple tasks to Sam whilst he worked like a Trojan at the harder or more complicated ones. But, there were times when he had to resort to stronger measures with Sam.

Penelope came downstairs one day to take a break from the boredom of painting and was just walking towards the kitchen when she heard a loud commotion coming from the parlor. She hurried to the room where she was faced with a scene straight out of a Marx Brothers movie!

Edward was doubled over with laughter (it was the first time she ever heard him laugh) while Sam swung slowly back and forth on the huge crystal chandelier - his feet missing the ladder under him by mere inches.

"What is going on here?" she asked.

"Mr. Ha! Ha! Mr. Ha! Ha! Mr. Sam climbed up there to fix the wiring on that old chandelier and the ladder slipped away ...Ha! Ha! Ha! he got himself stuck on the chandelier," Edward laughed breathlessly!

Penelope had to admit she was rather taken by the comic value of the situation. She soon joined Edward in gales of laughter as Sam swung helplessly back and forth like the pendulum of an old clock!

"Get me down from here," yelled Sam!

"OK," said Edward, "But only if you promise to get out of my hair and let me go on with my work!"

"Listen Edward, I'm the owner of this house and I'll do as I please!" answered Sam stubbornly.

"Suits me," said Edward, as he and Penelope turned to leave the room.

"OK, OK", shouted Sam, "you win. Just get me off this darn thing before I fall to the floor. I could break my neck you know!"

"Glad to oblige you, Mr. Sam," said Edward with an air of complete innocence.

As Penelope was walking towards her office she could hear the telephone ringing in the distance and rushed to answer it.

"This is Richard Taylor," the voice said. "I'm calling from Toronto. I would like to know whether you have decided to open your boarding house or not?"

"Well, Mr. Taylor," Penelope said. "What a surprise to hear from you. Yes, I have decided to convert my home into a boarding house but I won't be ready for a good seven weeks or so."

"This is fine with me, Mrs. Woodspring, since the negotiations on my land purchase are not finalized yet I don't plan to come to Victoria for the next two months. Would you reserve a place for me? I'll send you a deposit by mail tomorrow."

"That won't be necessary, Mr. Taylor, I'll hold a place for you," Penelope concluded.

After she hung up, Penelope realized that she was somewhat touched emotionally by that man's voice as well as his resemblance to her former lover. Yet, something inside was warning her to be careful about this individual!

***

That night she dreamt that a policeman who was chasing him for some reason or other had shot one of the boarders. Strangely enough the man in her dream resembled Jason McKee. At another point a lady boarder was involved in selling drugs in a downtown area. She was under constant police surveillance.

One of the policemen kept coming back to Penelope asking questions about the people who lived in her house. He said to her that he could not understand why a nice person like herself had such a weird group of people around her. When she tried to explain to the policeman that these people were only boarders, not relatives, his image kept fading away.

Further on in her dream she was sitting in court awaiting the beginning of the trial of one of the boarders, but when the judge hit his gavel on the desk she woke up in a sweat.

CHAPTER FOUR...

The RCMP surveillance team had noted the activity that was going on at Taylor's warehouse docking facility. They were keeping a close eye on Taylor himself. The night before departing for his fishing trip he had made several trips from the warehouse to the boat with what looked like bags of groceries. They saw him load his fishing equipment. Their instructions were to avoid detection at all costs. For that reason they stayed at a distance using night glasses to observe his movements. Inspector Woodchuck had ordered his men not to interfere with whatever Taylor did. They certainly didn't want to botch operation "Oceanside" by causing any suspicion when all the "big fishes" were close at hand. It was more important to halt this whole international operation than stop a small part that could easily be replicated in a different area.

The vessel on loan from the Coast Guard was ready to go into action at a moment's notice. The experienced pilot who came with it was certainly an added bonus for Woodchuk's team. Not having to worry about navigation was a great relief to the inspector and his men. The morning that Taylor set out, a telephone communication was urgently placed to the Inspector's office; "Operation Oceanside" was immediately put in motion.

Three experienced members of the narcotics team including Sergeant Harry Popleski joined the Coast Guard pilot and set out from Victoria Harbor to follow Taylor's boat. The Coast Guard vessel was camouflaged as a sport fishing boat, the men were dressed accordingly. They were all well armed with high-powered rifles and plenty of ammunition. They had plenty of food in addition to survival equipment aboard. All the official markings had been taken off the sides of the boat. A special radio channel had been installed, which would allow them to keep in constant touch with the Coast Guard/RCMP Headquarters without too much risk of anyone listening in. Inspector Woodchuck was able to monitor their movements and communications from his office in Victoria. In an emergency, they would be able to call in helicopter support with whatever else might be needed. The pilot of the Coast Guard "fishing boat" noticed that Taylor was not sailing towards the strait of Georgia but made a turn southwest into the strait of Juan de Fuca then north west toward Pachena Point.

Where possible Taylor's boat navigated within a couple of miles of the shoreline. They were probably going towards the north end of Vancouver Island before heading straight towards the Queen Charlotte Islands.

Fortunately there was a fair amount of coastal traffic including fishing boats, sailboats

and speedboats. This made it all easier for the
RCMP team to follow without being conspicuous.

All was going well for the first two hours
or so then suddenly, as often happens on the Pacific Ocean, the winds came up, the sea started to
swell and the rain came down in buckets. It became so rough that the pilot had to reduce the
speed. The two constables who were not the most
experienced boat going people, became seasick.
The wind had been blowing hard for about half an
hour when the pilot informed Sergeant Popleski
that Taylor's boat was nowhere to be seen. The
waves were swelling approximately ten to fifteen
feet, which seriously reduced their long distance
visibility. Popleski picked-up a set of powerful
binoculars. After a few minutes of searching, he
could see what looked like their quarry a mile or
so ahead. He immediately informed the boat's pilot. As quick as it had blown up, the winds died
down. The swell of the ocean subsided within
minutes. This was most welcomed by the two constables whose pale sweating faces regained a red-
der more windswept appearance. They had been
standing straining to see the horizon from the open
area of the bow of the boat. The pilot reported that
Taylor's boat had turned inland towards Tofino
and was instructed to follow.

Once they passed into the protected waters,
they saw that several sailboats as well as speedboats had also gone in to moor or anchor to shelter
from the angry sea. Quite slowly they went by
Taylor's boat. They all noticed that only the captain and a woman were on board. A couple of

hundred yards past Taylor's boat, they were able to dock without arousing suspicion. Popleski sent one of the young constables, who was new to the detachment to find out where Taylor might be. In the meantime, the rest of them decided to walk to a restaurant for a good cup of coffee.

When they arrived, they could see in an outside telephone kiosk the silhouette of a man who looked like Taylor. Popleski decided to approach the telephone booth pretending he wanted to make a call. He reached the kiosk door just as Taylor walked away from the telephone crossing the street to a small gift shop. Popleski went into the telephone booth in order to watch the gift shop across the street. After a ten to fifteen minutes wait, Taylor came out of the store with a large shopping bag, and then he walked to where his boat was docked. Right behind him came the young constable also carrying a small bag. The sergeant went to the restaurant to join the rest of the crew.

Popleski told his men that Taylor had made a telephone call to someone. He was having the Inspector check with the telephone company to find out where the call had been made. The young constable told everyone that he had not seen what Taylor purchased but saw that he paid over three hundred dollars in cash. However, going to the storeowner might compromise their undercover status. After their coffee and snack they ambled back to their boat, to keep close tabs on this international smuggler.

It's customary for boat people to wave to one another so, when they saw Taylor's boat go by them, the Pilot waved and the Captain returned the gesture. Sergeant Popleski as well as his men knew that Tom McMillan was privy to who they were and why they were there. They were also aware of the tremendous risk to which Captain McMillan and the lady were exposed. One wrong move would make them become fish bait! Popleski just knew that "the old sea Captain" would find a way to let them know where he was going. The Sergeant was impatient to know! The winds had died down making the sailing much easier, especially for the two constables with their "virgin sea legs."

***

Meanwhile in Victoria there had been some very important activities put forward by Inspector Michael J. Woodchuck's narcotics team. They had obtained a search warrant for Taylor's room at 13 Military Street in addition to the warehouse on the Gorge Waterway. They were very discreet in searching Taylor's suite. Officers only did so after talking with Sam and the housekeeper who were very upset. They were especially worried because Penelope was traveling with Taylor and would not return for another ten days. The Inspector told both of them that they were aware of Penelope's whereabouts. From their investigation they didn't think she had any involvement in this man's illegal operation. "As a matter of fact," the Inspector said, "no other person other than the two of you should know about this. I would request that you keep it confidential until we have completed our investigation as well as our search."

Sam and the housekeeper were really shaken by these events but both told the Inspector they would not tell a soul about the whole thing. "It was too upsetting," they said. Not knowing fully what was going on would only make people speculate and come up with wrong conclusions.

***

The search of Taylor's room only produced a notebook with names, local telephone numbers, as well as in Vancouver, Seattle, Toronto, Montreal, New York City, Bogota and Lebanon.

The warehouse search was a different proposition altogether. The employees had been given paid vacation time while the boss was away on his "fishing trip." This made the access easier for the Inspector and his men, without having to answer anyone's questions.

In the office desk used by Taylor, a locked drawer was forced open. They found what would turn out to be the key to locating the "special merchandise" they were looking for but did not realize it immediately. However, as they were searching, the Inspector himself didn't know what these coded messages meant.

After two days of searching they still had not found the merchandise they were looking for.

At one point, the Inspector thought the search was useless, that Taylor had succeeded in misleading the authorities. But knowing how these smugglers operated worldwide he knew somewhere in this warehouse the illegal drugs they were looking for were hidden! The question was where? They knew they had the right person as well as the right place, but had they come at the wrong time?

For years Richard Taylor, better known to the law enforcement agencies by his real name of Benjamin Malouf, had been the elusive importer of drugs from Colombia, South America as well as other parts of the world. These drugs would end up on the streets of North America.

Malouf's knowledge of international smuggling was superb. His ability to avoid being caught had been a thorn in the side of Interpol, the FBI and the RCMP. No other criminal in the world had so successfully avoided entrapment. He successfully thwarted charges against him by all law enforcement agencies of many jurisdictions involved. It was almost like this man lived a charmed life.

Well, obviously he had such a life for many years, but now finally there was a possibility of catching him red-handed. Inspector Woodchuck certainly didn't want to jeopardize his chances of being the law enforcement agency to do so.

He continued to search the warehouse looking into every crate or container, including the stocked merchandise on shelves. He hammered on the walls but nothing appeared to be out of the or-dinary.

The search team members were really frustrated at not finding any drugs anywhere. The Inspector went back to the log book found in the locked drawer of the office desk looking through it page by page trying to find a clue that would shed light on where the contraband could be hidden.

One page was written in Italian along with symbols of crossed bones crudely drawn - no enlightenment from that page.

On another page, this time written in French and Spanish there was also a design that appeared to be in the shape of a crucifix or a cross of some kind. There did not appear to be any relationship between the crude drawings and the different languages written on the page. While he was deep in thought about these symbols, a constable walked in carrying a statuette in each hand. The Inspector looked up and asked the young officer, somewhat impatiently, if there was a problem of some kind - that he should come in and interrupt his train of thoughts.

"I believe there is, Sir!" the constable answered. "You see these two items appear to be the same size, shape as well as the same design as I place them on the desk in front of you. But, as you lift them there seems to be a difference in weight!"

The Inspector lifted the statuettes to confirm that the one in his left hand seemed to be a bit heavier. As he turned them over he noticed that the one in his left hand had a crossed bones design on its base. He decided to smash the head against the side of the desk. To their surprise a small bag fell to the floor.

"Bingo," said the young constable, "we've found it!"

The Inspector told him to inform the other team members to bring all the small statuettes that had any type of markings on their bases to the office.

"There would not be enough room in here Sir," the young constable said. "You see there are some three hundred or more cases of these out there on the warehouse floor. Must have had a fire sale somewhere," he added jokingly.

"Well," said the Inspector, "let's go have a look at each case and take the items out one by one. Any that you find that have markings on the base, any kind of markings, place them aside until we have all the boxes opened." Woodchuck placed a call to headquarters to request more help.

Taylor was a dangerous criminal who had killed people, had people killed to protect his drug business. Every precaution would have to be taken to prevent the killing of innocent bystanders.

CHAPTER FIVE

It was just a little over two months since they had vigorously started to rehab the old mansion. Penelope thought the time was appropriate to hear from the advertisement for boarders that had been placed in the paper for just about two weeks now.

She was very thankful that Edward had come by to offer his services. Without him there was no doubt in her mind that Sam could not have accomplished alone what had been done. After the chandelier incident he had been very co-operative. He adjusted to the fact that Edward was a better, more knowledgeable worker than he.

Penelope had never been a morning person. But on this day, she got up early, proceeded to the kitchen to prepare breakfast for both Sam and herself. As soon as she entered the kitchen she realized that she would have to do battle with Count Dracula again. She thought that maybe the time had come to purchase a new modern electric or gas stove instead of having this antiquated piece of iron. There must be a good appliance store somewhere in Victoria. Penelope was just in the process of searching for the local paper to find out if any appliance sale was advertised, when the doorbell rang. It startled her. Since they had been renovating, for that matter since they had moved in, these were the first chimes to be heard!

As she opened the front door, she was greeted by a medium-size average-looking female with a ready smile. "Hi! My name is Felicity Potts. I'm here in answer to your advertisement for boarders!" She carried one of those handbags that bore a strong resemblance to a small suitcase. Near where she was standing were two large suitcases and a footlocker. Penelope's eyes registered dollar signs as she took all this in. Surely she was planning to be their first boarder, or she would not have brought this huge amount of luggage along.

"So glad to meet you, Mrs. Potts," Penelope said with real enthusiasm. "I'm Penelope Woodspring, the owner."

"Its Miss Potts, if you don't mind. Could I have a look around the house?"

"By all means, do come in and look around as much as you would like to," said Penelope eagerly.

Felicity stepped right in, proceeded down the hall and, for some reason unknown to Penelope, opened the kitchen door to obviously make a quick survey of the place. She then asked without even looking at the owner standing next to her, "You serve three meals a day here, don't you?"

"Why, of course," lied Penelope! "How could this be a boarding house without meals?"

Actually she had not planned to serve meals. Penelope had some vague notion that they would have some sort of community kitchen, where everyone would pitch-in and make a project out of each meal!

Opening the cupboards, seeing how bare they were, Felicity said; "You are going to have to fill these cupboards with supplies if you intend to feed a full house of people!"

"Oh! I know, I know," said Penelope in a soft voice. "Perhaps you could help me with planning the menu? That is, if it's not asking too much of your time?" With that remark and without knowing it, Penelope had just placed the proverbial foot in her mouth!

"Well, since you brought it up," said Felicity innocently, "I am a very good cook. I just might consider doing your cooking in return for a portion of my rent, if we can come to an agreement!"

"And what would you consider a good agreement?" asked Penelope just about feeling like a swimmer being drawn into a whirlpool!

"Why don't we discuss that at a later time, if I decide to stay here," said Felicity.

Throwing caution to the winds, Penelope asked in a nonchalant voice, "Did you ever cook on one of those? This old Dracula is quite a challenge for anyone."

"Are you kidding me," Felicity said laughing. "Why, I wouldn't have one of those puny modern stoves if I had to choose between...what did you call it again? Dracula! These old combination stoves are the only kind that is worth cooking on."

That answer did it. Penelope felt light-headed at the thought of someone taking that burden away from her. "I'm sure that we can come to a suitable agreement," she said. "That is if you decide to live in our house."

"Do you have a handyman around here," asked Felicity?

Penelope suppressed a laugh. "My brother Sam serves in that capacity."

"Would you mind having him put my bags in the maid's quarters?" Felicity asked.

"Certainly." Penelope left to find Sam. Running out into the hall she shouted, "Sam where are you?"

As soon as she saw him coming towards her, she ran up to him and whispered; "Go out on the porch, get all that luggage moved into the maid's quarters," she told him. "Take my belongings upstairs, use the back stairs and don't ask any questions!"

"But, but, but," he stammered.

"Don't ask any questions, and hurry!" she shouted at him. He moved off towards the verandah, mumbling under his breath, and Penelope raced back to the kitchen.

"What was all that shouting about?" Miss Potts asked.

"It's just that my brother Sam is sometimes a little hard of hearing, especially when it comes to work."

"I'm going to have to go shopping for food," said Felicity.

"But we have food in the refrigerator," Penelope began to say...

"All I found were TV dinners and instant coffee. Not very much to feed three healthy people with, would you not agree?"

"We have been very busy with the decorating as well as some major repairs, and I must admit my kitchen talents are extremely limited. Let me find my purse to give you money for the groceries. Sam can go with you, he's a very safe driver."

When she returned to the kitchen she saw that Felicity was whittling a stack of shavings with one of the butcher knives. She had picked some pieces of wood from a small pile in back of the stove. Penelope had often wondered what that wood was for!

As soon as Miss Potts had a generous pile of shavings ready, she stuffed them unceremoniously into Dracula's mouth, added a few pieces of coal and in a very short time had a roaring fire going. Penelope could hardly contain her amazement!

She left the kitchen again to go look for her brother to drive Felicity to the grocery store. She was just about to walk through the kitchen doors when she suddenly heard sobs coming from the dining room area. She hurried to the service room adjacent to the dining room and spied on Miss Potts standing there, her hands over her eyes and tears streaming down her face.

"Why, Miss Felicity," Penelope exclaimed! "What on earth is the matter, why are you crying so hard?" she asked.

"When you left the kitchen, I decided to take a second look at this beautiful dining room." With a softer voice she added, "Everything is just so lovely. These are the things I have been dreaming of all my life. When I was a child, we were so poor that we could only afford thick, ugly dime-store china with cheap utensils that anybody could buy at Woolworth's! You know, I never had a birthday party when I was a little girl. I was too embarrassed to have other kids come to our house to see the entire junky furniture and horrible dishes we had." Then, realizing she had let her guard down in a moment of weakness, she said gruffly, "I see that you've found your purse. Is your brother Sam ready to take me to the grocery store?"

Sam walked in on them at that very moment. Penelope introduced him to their first boarder and chef-to-be! "

I'm ready when you are, Miss Potts," he said. "The car is out front. You can't miss it. You'll know what I mean when you see it."

Felicity and Sam were gone for over an hour. When they returned with several bags of groceries, Miss Potts had totally recovered her brashness.

Looking at Penelope, she said, "Where's my room?"

With no hesitation Penelope asked Felicity to follow her down the hall to the maid's quarters.

After carefully surveying the place, Felicity said, "I guess it will do. Does that gas heater work?"

"Which gas heater?" Penelope gasped, momentarily forgetting that as the owner of this house she should know where things are!

"That one," replied Felicity, pointing to the ornate little metal cabinet in the corner.

"Why, why, I guess so," she said. "I've never tried it."

At least that was not a lie. Penelope had been very cold every night since moving into this beautiful house. That should not have happened at all. She really felt a bit stupid for not knowing what the corner metal cabinet was, suddenly realizing that having Felicity as a boarder was beginning to look like a good deal for her.

***

That night at the dining room table, they had their first meal. Having been a globetrotter, Penelope had dined in many world famous restaurants. This first boarding house meal could have been a credit to any first class chef anywhere. Her brother Sam agreed without hesitation!

After the main entrée, Penelope and Sam both thought that the meal had ended that the summit of taste ecstasy had been reached. They got another surprise when in came; "La pièce de résistance," a most beautiful pumped-up angel-food cake with homemade strawberry ice cream!

Penelope immediately thought that the thirty dollars she had given Felicity for groceries, was all spent on that one meal. She was dead wrong. Miss Potts soon started to initiate Penelope into the intricacies of economically operating a kitchen.

As the three of them were relaxing over a good cup of coffee, the doorbell rang and Penelope sprang to her feet to answer it.

"Just a minute," said Felicity, "I'm the maid here, and if there is any doorbell answering to do, I'll do it."

Penelope decided to accompany her to the front door anyway, since she did not have much faith in the "maid's diplomacy" at this early stage.

"Well," she heard her say in her best no-nonsense voice, "What can we do for you, my dear lady?"

She was speaking to a small woman who appeared to be in her seventies. Her small oval face, softly framed in wispy snow-white hair, resembled a fine antique cameo. She wore a soft mauve dress that was a bit long to be stylish and the kind of shoes older women are forced to wear because their feet are no longer as young as their minds! A thin cloth coat was drawn tightly around her frail body. She was taken aback by Felicity's overbearing air. The little woman appeared to be ready to turn around without saying anything.

"I came to inquire about a room you advertised," she said in a very soft pleasant voice. "My name is Eileen Flowers. I'm just about ready to leave the 'rest home' that my children had chosen for me. I can't stand listening to old people complain all day long! I simply have to find a place where I'll have peace of mind."

Penelope immediately realized that she needed to turn to Felicity for help.

"How much should I charge her?" she whispered to Miss Potts.

"Seventy-five dollars a week, in advance," she said emphatically.

As they were talking, Sam came into the hallway to see what was going on. Penelope was almost positive she detected a subtle change in Mrs. Flowers' attitude. Her shoulders seemed to straighten noticeably, her head was thrown back, and again Penelope thought she saw a faint gleam in the little old lady's fading blue eyes.

"Why, hello, young man," she said almost coquettish, "do you live here?"

"Yes I do," said Sam. "As a matter of fact I'm the landlady's brother. My name is Sam."

"In that case I'm sure I'll enjoy living here. How much did you say the room was?" Eileen asked turning to Penelope.

"Seventy-five dollars a week - in advance," replied Felicity.

"My, that certainly sounds reasonable," she said pulling a large wad of bills from her purse. Counting three hundred dollars she said, "I'll just pay you a month in advance," and handed the money to Penelope.

Penelope could see that Felicity was mentally berating herself for not making the rent somewhat higher. Miss Woodspring was too busy wondering why this nice little old lady had really left the rest home in a hurry, to be concerned about the amount of the rent. Furthermore, she was worried that this frail woman carried such a large amount of cash in her purse!

Eileen smiled sweetly, stepped aside, and looking directly at Sam said, "My bags are on the verandah. I'm sure a strong young man like you will find a way later on to bring them up to my room, won't you?"

Sam blushed like a schoolboy and stammered, "Why, why certainly ma'am."

"Now, I'm very tired," Eileen continued. "Suppose you show me up to my room!"

As she followed Sam up the stairs, Penelope could feel that something was very wrong with either her or Mrs. Flowers. She got the distinct impression that Eileen was slinking up the stairs after her brother.

Sam was gone for about ten minutes, then came running down the stairs all out of breath!

"That sweet little old lady is nuts," he panted.

"What on earth are you talking about?" his sister asked.

"As soon as we got up to the room," he replied indignantly, "she pulled off her coat, lay back on the bed and asked me to rub her ankles. Of course I thought nothing of that, until I started to rub one of her ankles. She grabbed me and told me what a strong handsome young man I was. To top it all, she tried to kiss me!"

"Oh, Sam," said Penelope, "I'm sure you must be imagining things! It was probably just a motherly kiss."

Penelope certainly was not ready to believe that Eileen was a seventy-year-old seductress. She realized that her brother Sam was highly imaginative.

"I'm telling you that old woman tried to vamp me," Sam insisted! "You don't look as if you believe me at all!"

"Listen, Sam," Penelope said impatiently, "I have a hard time believing this nice little old lady would turn out to be a person with loose morals or worse. If a man your age cannot protect himself from the amorous advances of a seventy-year old woman, you'll just have to suffer the consequences!"

"Well, all I can say is she better keep her hands off me or she'll be sorry," Sam replied peevishly.

"Ha! Ha! Ha!" laughed Felicity, "Sam has a very willing girl friend! Better not hug her too hard, honey, her brittle bones may break!"

"I don't need any sassy comments from anyone. If we're not more careful, this place is going to turn into a funny farm for elderly nuts!"

"All I have to say," added Penelope, "is that she appears like a perfectly normal sweet little old lady to me. Let's not have any more silly talk about her being on the make, until we find out more about who she is and where she really comes from. The breakfast table will certainly be a better place for a straightforward conversation."

"It's OK with me, but don't say that I didn't warn you," said Sam, as he moved towards the parlor.

Felicity just shook her head and kept on laughing all the way down the hall to the maid's quarters.

The boarding house was having a great beginning, or was it?

CHAPTER SIX…

Everything was coming along rather well since the arrival of the new boarders three weeks ago. Penelope had decided to move Sam's quarters to the guesthouse at the back of the old mansion. It had three bedrooms, three bathrooms and would be quite comfortable and private for male boarders. She was also thinking of Richard Taylor who had called again and said he was coming to Victoria soon.

The redecorating and repairs were completed, thanks to little old Edward the very talented handyman, as well as the efforts of her brother Sam. Penelope was sure that Edward had saved her a tremendous amount of money that she would otherwise have had to pay different trades people.

They were having breakfast one morning when suddenly the doorbell rang. A loud voice could be heard saying, "Is anyone going to answer this door?" Penelope did not stir, she had had a bad night. For some reason her dreams had taken her back to Havana and the discovery of Jason McKee's body. She had pushed the unpleasant incident almost out of her mind but obviously, not well enough. These kinds of dreams made her really tired and grouchy. Then, she would remember the good times and her bad humor would fade away.

"I suppose it's up to me to go and see what is happening at the door," said Felicity as she went through the dining room doors and down the hall.

Penelope decided to follow as she realized that Felicity could be abrasive if not rude with people she didn't like on first contact. She was in business now and could not afford to lose clients as well as get a bad reputation at the same time. It would be difficult enough to get boarders, without one having to apologize for someone else's behavior.

As Felicity opened the front door, Penelope could see a man in his early sixties standing there. Next to him stood a woman who could be described as an oddball or an artist. The man was very well dressed in a pin-stripe suit with an old fashioned double-breasted jacket. He had a look about him that said "gentleman." Although it had been raining, his Homburg looked as if it had just been brushed. His shiny black patent shoes completed his smart appearance. In looking at his face one could detect the thin straight nose, light blue steely eyes and tightly compressed lips that gave him a look of some severity.

The woman, on the other hand, was a bit chubby with a hard face. She wore a terrible black crêpe dress, of the type that went out of style in the late twenties. It was ankle length, and heavily encrusted with cheap glass beads that reminded one of the notions counter at a five and ten store.

Looking at these people, Penelope thought, what a strange couple these two are. Then, "Good morning," she said in a calm controlled voice, "how can I help you folks?"

"Madam, my name is Reginald Van Orsdal, I'm here to inquire about the sign in your yard regarding lodgings!"

"The hell you say," objected the woman. "No damn sissified man is going to cramp Joyce Mahoney's style. I saw the sign first. Just because you rang the doorbell ahead of me does not give you the privilege to have first choice. Do you understand that, mister fancy pants?"

Sensing some friction and realizing that these people were not a couple, Penelope immediately informed the man that the only quarters available for gentlemen were in the guesthouse at the back of the property. This seemed to calm Joyce Mahoney's aggressiveness for the time being.

"Felicity could you show Miss Mahoney the rooms we have available in the main house while I take the gentleman to the guesthouse?"

Penelope thought that this approach would ease the tension for the time being. It did, but not for very long. She invited Reginald Van Orsdal to follow her down the hall to the back of the house where she could show him the guest quarters. They were not five steps from the mansion when she could hear Joyce's voice complaining to Felicity about having to climb stairs and what not!

Some weeks ago Sam had moved to the guesthouse hoping to have peace of mind. Penelope explained the arrangements to Van Orsdal who made no immediate comments. The room she showed him was the largest one of the three, complete with private bath including a walk-in closet. She had carpeted the floor and had added some of the antiques from the main house. The room, in fair weather, was filled with sunlight all day long which made it very attractive, even to a male's eye!

"I guess it will suffice," said Reginald Van Orsdal, "but there are a few things we must agree upon before I move in! First, I'll require laundry services once a week along with fresh linen."

"Well"... Penelope stammered, completely flabbergasted by such demands! "This is not a hotel, my dear sir. We don't have room service. We only provide our boarders with the necessary linens, which one has to take care of on his or her own. All meals are served in the dining room of the main house at regular hours. If you wish a telephone you can order one from the telephone company under your own name using 13B Military Street, as the address. The cost will be seventy-five dollars a week."

She expected this gentleman to walk away without a word. To her surprise, he seemed to agree to the arrangements without any further comments just asking if it would be convenient for him to move in immediately. He proceeded to write Penelope a check for a full three months rent.

"Whom do I make the check payable to?" he asked.

"You can write it to me, Penelope Wood-spring, if you please, I'm the sole owner of this property."

She was still in a state of disbelief when, on the way back to the mansion, she ran into Felicity who did not appear to be very happy about having had to deal with the boisterous Joyce Mahoney.

"So," she said, "did mister fancy pants decide to stay on with us or are we too far below his standards for the 'gentleman' to consider?"

Without giving her any details, Penelope told Felicity that Mr. Van Orsdal had accepted the terms. "I explained to him what the dining room rules were and he just went along with it all. I don't understand why you're so negative about people! We should not judge if we don't want to be judged."

"Well," said Felicity, "I thought that he would try to pull the wool over your eyes in order to get all kinds of privileges that other boarders won't have. That in itself would have been a real problem. I'm glad you showed your authority without giving into his 'hoity-toity' way of speaking!"

Penelope privately thought just how right Felicity had been in her assessment of Van Orsdal.

"Now," she said, "let's get Miss Mahoney settled so that we can get on with what it is we have to do!"

As they entered the parlor a scene of absolute tranquility greeted them! Joyce Mahoney was sitting at the old upright piano, Sam and Miss Flowers were seated nearby. As it always was with Penelope, the things she worried about the most solved themselves easily.

Joyce Mahoney was banging away at the piano keys singing old songs of the Charleston era and even further back. For a woman, her voice sounded more like a tenor's. "Come on in, ladies," she belted out, hardly missing a note. "I was just giving these folks a little sample of how I used to knock 'em dead at the old New Frontier Saloon! Just reminiscing brings back such wonderful memories," Joyce said. She stopped playing right then and one could see the wetness in her big blue eyes!

"Where is, or should I say was, the New Frontier Saloon?" asked Penelope.

"That," said Joyce, "was in the Yukon Territory. I was brought up in that part of the world. Cold it was, and tough you had to be in order to survive."

Penelope figured that Miss Mahoney must be in her middle to late forties, no doubt ten years older than she.

"My parents brought me across the Chilkoot Pass when I was just a baby," said Joyce. "Of course, I don't remember a damn thing about it, but my father told me later on that it was cold enough going through that pass to freeze a well-digger's behind. Mom and Dad were not the lucky type, they never made it easy for themselves. Both died when I was fifteen leaving me without a dime. I was kicked around from pillar to post for a few years, washing dishes in a restaurant, sometimes playing-up to lonesome miners on the side for a few extra dollars."

Penelope noticed that Eileen got a strange look in her eyes from listening to Joyce's story, but she couldn't tell if it was shock or envy!

Joyce just kept on going with her story. She seemed to appreciate the attention the others were showing her.

Miss Mahoney continued, "When I was eighteen with a nice pair of legs as well as a fair-size set of endowments, I decided to get myself hired on as a so-called dance hall girl at the New Frontier Saloon where I thought the money would be better. After a little endowment pinching session with the owner, I got myself hired on. I then set out to make my mark in the world. Later on, I found out about this dried-up old maid, a school-teacher in town who gave piano lessons for a small fee. I took a few lessons, just enough, to enable me to bang out a few tunes on the old player piano in the saloon. Before you could say 'Jack-in-the-box' I was the featured entertainer in the place. I bought myself a few skimpy little costumes to move around among the customers, get a few pinches, and excited them so they would buy more drinks for which I got a cut. I then played a few tunes to keep them all happy. This was as far as I would go. The customers were always very drunk. They usually passed out on the cheap whisky that was served. Once I had collected my cut from the owner, I went home with my virtue intact!"

Penelope was a bit surprised that someone would openly tell most of their life story to a group of total strangers. She also noticed that as Joyce ended her last statement, Eileen appeared to be somewhat disappointed!

Worn out from her long narrative, but nevertheless pleased with herself for having made a shocking impression on the other guests, Joyce rose from her chair, yawned and said; "That's enough about me right now, would you kindly show me my room, Miss Woodspring?"

Penelope led the way upstairs to one of the best rooms in the house and at the same time the furthest away from her own quarters. She had the feeling that this person would, for some reason, snore heavily and loudly.

"This is a very lovely room," said Penelope in a kind of guilty tone. "Looking out the window you have quite a view of the Victoria Harbor front. On a clear day you can almost see the American shoreline," she added.

As Penelope took a step back to let Miss Mahoney get a feeling for her new quarters, Joyce asked, "Is there any heat in this cubbyhole?"

"Why...yes?" said Penelope in a sharp tone as she reached over to light the gas heater, which was in the fireplace.

"Oh hell," snapped Joyce, "I didn't mean for you to light it right now. The temperature is just about right at this time."

Penelope watched nervously as Joyce looked around with a critical eye plunking herself down on the old bed. The bed groaned a bit, but that was to be expected with old furniture however massive the piece.

"You don't mind if I call you Penny, do you? After all, you are a few years younger than I am, are you not? I just turned 48 three weeks ago, doesn't feel a day over 40. How about you?"

"Well, you are asking rather personal questions. For your information I would rather be addressed by my full name which, as you know, is Penelope."

"Miss Penelope," mimicked Joyce in a higher tone of voice, "how much are you going to charge me?"

"Seventy five-dollars a week in advance," said Penelope. "Does that meet with your budget requirements Miss Mahoney?"

"Sounds reasonable enough," said Joyce suddenly softening her tone of voice. She opened her purse handing Penelope two one hundred and five twenty-dollar bills, saying that she could give her a receipt later. "Is there someone who could bring my bags up? I'm really bushed and would like to rest a bit before lunch."

"Of course," said Penelope "I'll have my brother Sam bring your luggage up when I get back downstairs."

"Before you go, I would like to know if I can roam around this big house, without opening doors of course, or am I confined to quarters?"

"Of course you're not confined to quarters," Penelope answered with genuine sincerity. "We are family here and we act the part, I hope. You can have a look at all floors but I would advise you to stay out of the kitchen. You see, Felicity is a wonderful cook but she does not like anyone to interfere with the way she has her 'cuisine' set out. Even I gladly stay out of her way!"

"Thanks, for the information, Miss Woodspring. Please let me know when you would like some light entertainment, I'll be glad to oblige."

As she made her way back downstairs, Penelope had mixed emotions about this oddball, strange woman. At the same time she felt some admiration for someone who had such rugged independence as well as uncompromising bluntness.

Lost in her thoughts, she almost bumped into Felicity who was standing in the hallway, hands on hips. "Well," Felicity said, "did you not even try to discourage the old bat from boarding here?"

"No, I did not try to discourage her," said Penelope, "and neither will you! She's a paying guest in this house, which you should not forget! Besides, I would appreciate if you did address her by her name and not old bat!"

Felicity turned on her heels literally running towards the kitchen, muttering under her breath all the way.

Penelope was sorry she had been so abrupt with Felicity but she also felt that she must be fair to everyone living here, including the kitchen staff. After all, she was getting a fair deal along with free lodging.

As she turned wearily towards the parlor, she saw Eileen standing in the doorway in a somewhat seductive manner, or so she thought! She saw that she was motioning with one finger towards Sam who was trying to walk to the library.

"Something wrong with your finger Miss Flowers," snapped Penelope?

"Why...why...no," answered Eileen, "just a touch of arthritis." And she retreated quickly up the stairs!

"Sam," called Penelope, "Miss Mahoney would like to have her luggage taken to her room. Would you be kind enough to do that?"

"Well, at least I won't have to be worried about being attacked by an over-sexed old woman," he answered sharply as he proceeded to get Miss Mahoney's luggage from the verandah.

Penelope walked into the library and sank her tired bones into a fat comfortable leather chair, while reflecting on the morning's events. It appeared as if it would be a long fall season in addition to a longer winter. Between having to keep Eileen away from Sam, Joyce and Felicity out of firing range of each other, Joyce out of Mr. Van Orsdal's hair and vice-versa, she was going to be busier than a mother dog with six pups and five breasts!

Gathering up her courage, she headed for the kitchen to have a talk with Felicity. It appeared that as the head of this boarding house, Penelope had been permanently cast in the role of peace-maker. As she entered the kitchen, she heard Felicity banging pots and pans, rushing back and forth as if the whole place was on fire!

"Are you trying to get a week's work done in one day?" Penelope asked in a pleasant tone.

"No, not really," said Felicity. "It just is not my kind of day today, plus I have to prepare a quick lunch so that everyone will be kept happy. Isn't that what you expect out of me? If you get more boarders, I'm going to need some help in the kitchen, like a 'marmiton' for instance. I'm not complaining, on the contrary I'm very happy for you that people are moving in. We'll soon have a full house if it keeps going this way. Maybe you should think of canceling your advertisement in the Daily Colonist!"

"What's a marmiton?" asked Penelope.

"Just a kitchen helper, someone to wash the dishes, pots and pans, whatever else needs to get done," said Felicity. "It's an expression my mother used when I was a little girl. I always wanted to be of help in the kitchen. She would say, 'so you want to be my marmiton today."

"So," said Penelope, "your mother must have had some French influence in her background. I'm sure from what you say that she must have been a very fine warmhearted lady."

Tears filled Felicity's eyes. She was so choked-up, she couldn't comment any more!

Penelope went on, "I may have to place an ad in the paper to get you someone, unless you already have a person in mind, my dear!"

"Let's talk about that later," Felicity said. "Right now I have to put a quick lunch together for these hungry boarders, then prepare some dinner for tonight."

"What did you have in mind for dinner?" Penelope asked. "Maybe I could go do some shopping if necessary, or we could send Sam out!"

"No need for that my dear lady, I already did the shopping as Sam was kind enough to drive me to the store and back. Tonight we shall have; chicken and stuff! And that is all I'll say about it."

Since it was getting close to noon, Penelope decided to get out of the kitchen area so that the "chef" could get her work done. That did not prevent her from being a bit nervous, as this kind of domestic arrangement was all very new to her. Hopefully people will get along with one another when they sit down for meals. "A boarding house." what in the world possessed her to get involved in such a scheme!

Could it be the influence of the past fifteen years with Jason McKee with his "projects." *Well,* she thought, *time will tell if I made the right decision or not. For the time being I'll just have to wing-it, as people say.*

***

When lunchtime came, the guests were directed to the parlor where they found an assortment of sandwiches as well as cakes along with coffee and tea all set out on the beautiful coffee table. They were all invited to help themselves, as this was their first time together. They were informed by Felicity to look forward to a somewhat more formal dinner in the dining room that evening.

Around six or so, Penelope was just about to enter the kitchen when she heard the chef scream, "Stay out of here whoever you are, I'm very busy and don't need to be disturbed at this time!" Penelope turned on her heels to enter the dining room just as the guests were starting to arrive. She told them to take up any seat they wish around the table. With fourteen place settings there was more than enough room for everyone.

They were all sitting, chatting with one another when Felicity entered the room carrying a relish tray. There soon became an air of festivity in the dining room. Reginald Van Orsdal actually smiled a little when Eileen Flowers told him that he had lovely gray hair.

"Of course," she informed him, "mine is prematurely gray."

Felicity staggered into the dining room with a large platter of chicken stacked as high as Mount Baker.

Everyone had nothing but praise for the wonderful meal that Felicity had prepared for them; even Joyce made some comments about the fabulous apple pie. Felicity just stood there, uncomfortable with the compliments. Mr. Van Orsdal in addressing Joyce said, "Madam, though your mode of expression leaves much to be desired, I have to agree with you this is one repast at which it has been my pleasure to partake."

"Damn that man," said Joyce looking straight at Van Orsdal. She told him that he was the biggest windbag she had ever run into!

"Oh my," simpered Eileen, batting her eyelashes. "I think Mr. Van Orsdal just talks beautifully, don't you, Sam dear?"

"Oh yes," said Sam "just like a Latin teacher I had in school. I could never understand a word, but it was said that he was a very intelligent person."

Sensing an argument, Penelope said hurriedly, "I'm glad that you all enjoyed the meal, moreover I'm sure that Felicity is very grateful!"

Joyce got up to bid goodnight to everyone. "It has been a long day for me and I shall retire to my room early!"

Eileen got up mentioning that she needed her beauty sleep while looking at Sam with a smile on her face.

"I'm not tired yet," said Sam. "I think that I'll go into the library to watch television for a while. There is an old Boris Karloff movie on tonight, you know!"

"It looks as if we're left to ourselves," said Penelope to Reginald Van Orsdal. "I do hope that you'll enjoy living here. You can rest assured that I'll do my best to make your stay as pleasant as can be. There are always differences amongst the guests but they'll iron themselves out."

"I doubt that there is an iron strong enough to press a dent in Miss Mahoney," he said, "but I feel quite at home otherwise. Of course, I would be much happier if you could provide meals in the room as well as having linen service available."

"I'm sorry, but that is Felicity's department. Believe me I certainly wouldn't want to interfere in her household affairs," Penelope said.

"I'm not quite ready to tackle her yet," he said with an air of confidence, "however I'm sure that sooner or later she'll come around. I pride myself on having quite an effect on the fairer sex. Now I'll bid you good evening, my dear lady, and hope that you have a restful night. I have to catch-up on some reading. I have been entertaining myself with 'The Rise and Fall of The Roman Empire.' I'm no further than the third volume." He then got up to proceed to the gentlemen's quarters.

***

Penelope was quite pleased. The evening had gone fairly well considering the cast of characters involved. This boarding house business was going to be a challenge. For the time being, she did not mind at all. It kept her busy so that she didn't have to think about being without a companion.

Everyone seemed to have enjoyed the meal immensely. Penelope got up from the table and took a walk towards the kitchen.

"Felicity," she said as she entered, "I want to thank you for putting together such a feast. It kind of set the tone for the whole evening aside from placing everyone in a good mood. Maybe now is the time to talk about that suitable agreement that I mentioned the other day! First, I have a small shall I call it 'bonus' for you!" giving Felicity a crisp $50.00 bill.

"Since you're going to live here doing the kitchen work as well as the maid's duties, I think that we should get someone to help you. We're already six people including three regular boarders, already creating lots of work. I would like to get three or four more boarders, so that we have a fully operational business. I'd like to leave some rooms empty for now, but available if needed. You see, Felicity, from what I understand, Victoria has a very active tourist season. We could make those rooms available at a higher price, don't you think?"

Felicity didn't seem at all surprised. First she thanked Penelope for the bonus then went on to say; "Yes, we should talk about the duties that I have to do in order to agree on a monetary arrangement that will be satisfactory to both of us. "Did you have anything in mind as to what you would like to offer me?" asked Felicity.

Penelope thought for a moment, sat down to tell Felicity that her offer, if she approved, would include room and board with eighty dollars weekly for her work as chef and maid. Since the cooking would increase with the number of additional boarders, she would put an advertisement in the Daily Colonist for a 'marmiton' as Felicity had suggested! "Does that sound fair to you?" she asked.

"You don't need to place an ad in the paper," Felicity said. "I know of someone who would probably work with me for a few dollars, the experience, as well as her meals. Besides, she lives in town with her parents. The rest of your proposition sounds good to me, so let's shake hands on it like business people do."

Penelope was quite pleased that she had secured a very important part of her growing operation. She couldn't have done it by herself. Cooking was certainly not one of her best qualities. As she wandered into the library to see what Sam was up to, she saw that he was fast asleep in one of the big chairs. She decided to sit herself down, let her mind flow with the movie that was on television. It was one of those old horror movies, but it seemed quite relaxing after her busy day. Penelope got completely engrossed in it.

Then, just as the movie was reaching its most exciting part, Sam leaped up and shouted, "Get your hands off me, you old bat, I am not coming into your room now or ever!"

"Good grief, Sam, you scared me out of my wits!" shouted Penelope, getting to her feet. "What on earth is wrong with you?" "Huh," mumbled Sam sleepily. "Oh!, it's you Penelope." Gosh, I was having this awful nightmare, where Mrs. Flowers was trying to drag me into her room!"

"For heaven's sake, Sam, you're becoming obsessed about that poor little old woman," teased Penelope. "In the first place she doesn't have the strength to drag you in her room, secondly if she did get you in there, about the wildest thing she would want you to do would be to have tea and talk with her."

"Well, you think what you like," said Sam, "but I'm telling you, that old bag is after me. Personally, I think she's a senior citizen nymphomaniac, if there is such a beast."

"A nymphomaniac!" Penelope shouted with laughter. "Really, Sam, you're a scream! It's almost as bad as accusing Grandma Moses of painting pornographic pictures!"

"Oh, nuts," said Sam, "I'm going to bed, I can see that I won't get any sympathy from you."

He stalked out of the library; Penelope sighed as she went back to watching television and the end of the horror film. She was just about to doze off when Felicity came into the room.

"Boy, am I beat," said Felicity yawning. "I have not seen that many dirty dishes in a long while. Reminds me of threshing time back on the farm!"

"Oh," said Penelope, seeing her chance to draw Felicity out a little, "did you spend your childhood on a farm?"

"Never mind childhood!" said Felicity. "What childhood! I spent my first twenty years or so on the family farm in Saskatchewan. I started working at dawn and doing chores before I was hardly big enough to reach the top of the kitchen table. By the time I was thirteen, I was out in the fields every day from spring to late fall.

"My father was a kind of quiet man who expected each and every one of us to carry their load. Mind you I was the last of ten, four girls and six boys. Farming was not an easy life, besides, my father was a worrier, which did not help his moods. Not that he was mean or anything like that, he didn't have much time for complimenting anybody.

"My mother, on the other hand, was tiny, even kind of fragile but very warm hearted. She always had a hug for me and kind words to go with it. Working on the farm with my brothers made me tough. Being a girl did not make a difference to them. I had to do as much hard work as they did. They often teased me so much that I would get real angry and throw whatever I could get my hands on at them!

"Eventually they all left the farm, my older sisters were the first to go. They thought that getting married would make life easier for them. They all had five or six children of their own, I lost count somehow, there were so many of them. The work on the farm became too much for my father and myself.

"One day, as he and I were working together he said, 'Felicity, you should find yourself a good man and start your own family. I have been thinking about selling the place and retiring. Your mother could certainly use the rest. I'm not as energetic as I used to be.' I wasn't surprised by his comments because I had noticed his progressive lack of enthusiasm! After saying all this, he turned to walk towards the barn. I noticed that he put his right hand to his chest and then fell to the ground. I screamed but he didn't answer me, he had died of a massive heart attack.

"After the funeral we sold the farm. My mother and I moved to Regina, the nearest city to us. I wanted my mother to have some pleasures in her late life that she hadn't had on the farm. We bought a small house, because I was able to put a good meal together the idea of catering for people came to me.

"For the next fifteen years, I worked in every fancy home in the city, preparing dinner parties. My services were quite in demand. By reading anything that had to do with food preparation, I taught myself to cook and create just about anything you could think of. As I got better, my business grew and so did my prices. I was able to care very well for my mother. I just didn't have much time for men. Except for Charles Tobin who always came around to check on mother and me."

"He was a good man; we were very good friends. With time we became lovers. My mother seemed to favor Charles more than anyone I had ever known. He was three years older than I but had the attitude in addition to the stamina of a twenty five-year-old. Living half a block down the street from us he was also a great help to me. Whenever I knew I was going to be very late coming home, I would ask him to make at least one check on mother to see that all was well. Very dependable, never complaining, always willing to do the things I wanted him to do, that was Charles.

"Then one day, after catering for a family hosting twenty guests, I came home late to find the lights on, a police car at the curb in front of the house. I knew in my heart that something had happened to mother. Charles rushed down the three steps of the verandah when he saw me approach. He just held me in a long hard hug."

"'Yes my sweet,' he said, 'your mother has died. When I came by to check on her and got no answer from the doorbell, I used my key to walk in. I found her lying on the couch as if sound asleep. I immediately called the ambulance. They tried to revive her without success. I'm very sorry,' he said with tears in his eyes." Felicity stopped as if reliving that moment, then she gabbled on (once started she wouldn't or couldn't stop). "For the next two months I refused all the work offers that came to me. I was depressed, feeling sorry for myself; I really missed my mother's companionship. Then I started doing some work again. Taking on as much as I could to keep busy, not have to think about life itself. Through all this time Charles was the most understanding person you could have around. He eventually moved in with me. Then one day, about six months ago as I was rocking on my verandah, a police car stopped in front of the house. I immediately got a woozy feeling in the pit of my stomach. Two officers walked up to me; the female policewoman asked me if I was Felicity Potts.

"'I sure am, what can I do for you officers?'" I answered.

"'We're very sorry madam, but have to inform you that Mr. Charles Tobin, who lived here, was killed by a drunk driver about two hours ago'.

"That, my dear Penelope, was about all I could take in sadness from one city. All my good memories were gone. I decided to sell the house with its contents, except for a few very personal possessions. I packed, got myself a plane ticket and came to Victoria.

"I just relaxed since moving here, not really knowing anyone nor what to do for that matter. I had walked by your beautiful house several times in the past two months. Then one day, as I was reading the local paper I saw your advertisement for boarders. From that point on I had a hunch that you might be in need of help. I didn't need a place to live but took a chance anyway. I just had to get myself back into the world of the living." Felicity finally paused.

"You'll never know how right that hunch of yours was," said Penelope. "You've only been here a very short time and I feel as if I have known you all my life."

"Enough of that," said Felicity, appearing very embarrassed for having opened up like she had. It had made her feel better to have shared with someone whom she thought would understand.

"I had better go to bed for my beauty rest if I want to be up bright and early for these hungry boarders we now have. I'm sure that old Van Orsdal will expect 'eggs benedict' or some other fancy breakfast item."

"Please Felicity, don't try so hard," said Penelope. "No one expects you to work yourself to death. I, for one, appreciate all that you are doing as well as the others."

Felicity got up, said 'goodnight' and then walked down the hall to her quarters.

Penelope just put her head back for a moment and thought over the events of the day. *It seems that I have collected a group of people with real problems instead of having a home for ancient nuts, as Sam suspected at first!*

There was something about Eileen Flowers that she couldn't put her finger on. Then her thoughts shifted to Richard Taylor who should be returning to Victoria soon to possibly take quarters in her boarding house. Again her whole inside seemed to be bothered by the simple thoughts of this man. Yet, her sub-conscience was giving her some warning signals!

Who is this Richard Taylor? Why does he disturb me so much? Many questions that remained unanswered for the time being.

CHAPTER SEVEN...

Joyce Mahoney tossed restlessly in her sleep then awoke suddenly when she heard Penelope come up the stairs. She took a quick look at her alarm clock to see the digits showing 12.30 a.m. She started to think about the delicious meal they had at dinnertime, it made her real hungry. She tried to go back to sleep but her thoughts kept returning to the chicken platter. She said to herself; I wonder if there is any of that good chicken left over?

Her mind wandered some more as she started to think about all the people living in this old house. *That Eileen is sure a queer one, eighty-five if she's a day, chasing Sam all over the place, like a schoolgirl! A woman her age should not be thinking about men, much less play with them! She should go after an older one like fancy pants Van Orsdal. He certainly would not be able to run away. Eh!* that's a thought, maybe I can get something going there!

What time is it? She turned towards her night table. *One o'clock in the morning finding myself wide-awake and hungry. I had better get up, sneak downstairs to get me a small piece of that chicken along with a glass of milk. That should tide me over until breakfast anyway.*

She got out of bed, put on her large fur slippers as well as her bathrobe and proceeded to the end of the hall. As she started to go down, she tested each step with her weight to make sure they would not creak taking the risk to wake someone up, especially Felicity. *Better let the "tigress" sleep tonight!*

As she came down the hall she could smell something like rotten eggs. As she got closer to Felicity's quarters, the smell intensified. She entered the room, immediately could smell that it came from a corner cabinet. She walked slowly towards it realizing that it was a gas heater turned on without a flame burning. She immediately turned it off, looked towards the bed and saw that Felicity was sound asleep breathing properly. On her way out she left the door slightly ajar so that the gas fumes or whatever that smell was, could get out.

She kept walking down the hallway towards the kitchen, found the door unlocked, walked in and turned the lights on to see where things were. She got herself a chicken leg along with a piece of apple pie in addition to a glass of milk then proceeded back to her room not even concerned anymore about the creaking stairs!

Once back in her room she told herself that she would have to make up a story to tell them in the morning hopefully not to raise any doubts about what she was doing downstairs in the middle of the night!

***

The next morning as Joyce was coming out of her room; she saw Penelope walking ahead of her. She called for her to wait a moment as she had something very important to tell her.

Penelope was stunned when she heard what happened. "My God," she said, "if you had not been taking a walk to the verandah, got lost in the dark, who knows what could have happened. I'm very grateful to you for that Joyce!"

"Oh, don't mention it," she said. "I'm glad it was not any more serious than that." *If you only knew,* she thought!

"I must call the gas company this morning to have them test all the heaters everywhere in the house," said Penelope as they entered the dining room.

They were the first ones to arrive for breakfast. The table was set with coffee and tea in large thermos servers in the center of the table.

Felicity walked in, offered everyone a choice of bacon and eggs or French toast or both if their appetite could take it!

***

"You look somewhat under the weather, my dear Felicity," said Penelope. "Have you not slept well?"

"Since you ask," Felicity said "I woke up with an awful headache. I didn't remember that I had left my door partly open. Not that there is any danger but one must be careful at all times."

"Do you remember turning your gas heater on last night?" asked Penelope. "Or did you just forget to light it for some reason or other".

"Oh! My Gosh," Felicity said. "You know I did a very stupid thing that I hope I'll never do again. I was so tired last night when I went to my room, closed the door, turned the gas heater on, went looking for matches, which I never found, totally forgetting I had left the heater turned on unlit!"

"Well," said Penelope, "you can be thankful to Joyce here who smelled the gas, followed her nose to your room and turned it off."

Felicity was stunned by these facts but grateful that she was still alive even though the "old bat" was not her favorite person.

***

Just as Felicity was going to tell them about the missing food from the refrigerator, in walked Sam followed by Reginald Van Orsdal and Miss Flowers. They all took a seat around the table helping themselves to tea or coffee. Felicity thought better, deciding to wait 'til another time to talk about someone taking food from the kitchen in the middle of the night. Before returning to the kitchen she approached Joyce quietly thanking her for turning off her unlit heater.

"What happened?" Eileen inquired! "Did someone do something wrong? Felicity looks a bit distressed this morning, is she not feeling well."

"All is fine now," answered Penelope. "It was just a minor mishap. I would ask each one of you to be very careful with the gas heaters in your rooms. Anyway I'm going to have them all checked by the gas company today, so please don't lock your doors if you go out of the house. Sam and I will be here all day; there is no need to worry about anything."

They had all received their breakfast food and were all attentive to what had just been said when Van Orsdal asked Joyce if she would like to have another piece of bacon

"Well," answered Joyce, "that is very generous of you. Are you on a diet? Or are you just making sure you stay fit and healthy? I do appreciate your gesture Mr. Van Orsdal; I will gladly take it, thank you very much."

Everyone was somewhat surprised by the gentleness and friendliness Reginald Van Orsdal was showing towards Joyce. For Penelope, this was only part of the old fox's way to impress and she was not at all fooled by it.

The door chimes rang which made Penelope get up to see who was there so early in the morning.

She opened the door to find Richard Taylor standing there. Penelope was still bothered by this man's close resemblance to Jason McKee. He could pass for his twin brother she thought.

"Good morning Mr. Taylor, when did you come back?"

"My plane landed just about an hour ago. I thought I'd come here first to check with you on available quarters before going to my hotel."

"I did reserve a suite in our guesthouse. If you would like to follow me I'll show it to you."

Taylor looked at the large room, which was well decorated, as well as being tastily furnished. It had its own bathroom, a bonus he had not expected.

"I'll take it," he said. "How much is it?"

"Seventy-five dollars a week, if you don't mind, that includes three meals a day. You'll have to walk over to the old mansion and join everyone in the main dining room for meals," she responded. "Linens are supplied but you have to take care of your own laundry. If you require a telephone you'll also have to make your own arrangements with the Phone Company using 13B Military Street as your address."

"That all sounds very good to me, Mrs. Woodspring. When can I move in?" he said with enthusiasm.

"It's ready for you right now. I'll give you a set of keys so that you don't have to bother anyone," Penelope replied.

He handed her $900.00 in cash saying; "I can see that it's going to be peaceful around here. How many boarders do you have?"

Penelope answered, "In this guest house there will only be three of you, my brother Sam as well as Reginald Van Orsdal, an older retired gentleman. Would you like to have a cup of coffee with us in the dining room and meet the other guests?"

"Thank you very much, Mrs. Woodspring, but not at this time. I have to meet with the real estate people who are handling a business property deal for me, then with the bank manager as well as a contractor I hired to build my warehouse," said Jason's look-alike.

Not only does he look good, she thought, *but he also has money if he can afford to pay his keep three months ahead of time.*

* * *

She returned to the dining room to find everyone still sitting around the table chatting away. "Well, ladies and gentlemen, that includes you Sam, we have a new boarder, a Mr. Richard Taylor, who's opening up a new business in Victoria. He will be the last addition to our guesthouse. I can assure you, Mr. Van Orsdal, that you'll not even hear him come and go. He appears to be a very nice gentleman as well; anyway, that is my opinion. You'll all have a chance to meet him at dinner tonight."

"What kind of business is he in," asked Eileen?

"Well," said Joyce, with tongue in cheek, "he might be the master of the house! Who knows!"

"What do you mean by that?" asked Eileen!

"I think that we should wait until we meet someone, who is going to live here with us, before making up any gossip about whatever they are or do," said Penelope.

She did not appreciate the fact that Joyce might have detected a slight change in her tone of voice when she spoke about the new boarder. She blushed a bit as she walked out of the dining room towards the kitchen to see how Felicity was feeling.

"I'm just here to check on you. Has your headache gone away? I hope you'll be more careful with the gas heater in the future. It can be deadly, you know," she added with some concern. "It seems to me that you were about to say something to us earlier in the dining room. Did something go wrong somewhere or what?" asked Penelope.

"Let me tell you what I found," said Felicity. "When I opened the refrigerator this morning, missing food that's what I found to be wrong. Someone in this house took the liberty of taking leftover food without asking me which I don't like. Am I going to have to padlock my kitchen?

"I have a feeling that Joyce might be the guilty one, but can't prove it. So, I thought better of it and kept my mouth shut. Was I glad after hearing about my own stupidity? On the other hand, it could be someone else. Do you think that it would be a good idea to have a lock put on the kitchen door or have some mechanism installed to block the dining-room service doors from opening?"

"It does not appear to be that serious yet! A first incident may not be repeated," said Penelope. "Anyhow as you were talking, I was just thinking that at dinner tonight I could make an announcement and inform our guests that the kitchen is not to be visited after 10 PM. If anyone feels that they need a late snack, all they have to do is ask! Would you agree with that, Felicity?"

"It sounds good to me," she said, "moreover it might just save us or should I say me, a whole lot of unnecessary aggravation."

"Let's try that approach and see if it works, added Felicity. Since our numbers are increasing, I'm going to do some food shopping today. Are you or Sam available to drive me to the store?

"I'm sure that one of us can," said Penelope. "I had better get on the telephone to the Gas Company to have all our gas outlets checked. I'll feel better if this is done right away."

She left the kitchen heading towards the library where, in one of the corners, Penelope had put a small antique desk with chair for her to use the telephone to tend her business as well as private calls.

As she was sitting at the desk undisturbed, the image of Richard Taylor came into her mind. She had never thought that anyone would arouse her feelings again as this man had done. His looks reminded her so much of Jason.

She wondered what he was like, her curiosity was aroused. Obviously she was missing the companionship of a lover but certainly did not want to fall head over heels with anyone. She was curious about the kind of business he was in! *Very well-dressed, drives a new car with a powerful engine. Did he run away from a nagging wife? Is he a widower?* So many questions left with no answers.

The ringing of the telephone startled her out of her rêverie. It was the gas company service man inquiring if someone would be home within the next half-hour! She assured him there would be. Getting all the gas outlets checked was her first priority of the day. She certainly didn't want a catastrophic accident which, first of all, would be terrible and secondly, could harm her new venture. She made a mental note to ask the gas serviceman about a possible safety valve of some kind that could be installed, which would automatically shut off the gas flow if it were not lit!

Still her thoughts could not stray far away from Richard Taylor. What kind of magnetism did this man have to cause such an effect on her?

CHAPTER EIGHT...

That evening when everyone had arrived in the dining room, Penelope introduced the new boarder. "Ladies and gentlemen this is Richard Taylor who will be the new addition to our growing family. Mr. Taylor, standing behind you is our wonderful chef Felicity, to your right is Reginald Van Orsdal, next to him is my brother Sam. Further down is Miss Joyce Mahoney and next to her is Miss Eileen Flowers."

Richard smiled at everyone as he told them that he was very happy to be part of the group and looked forward to getting to know all of them as the weeks went by. He waited until Penelope was seated before sitting down himself.

The conversations flowed pleasantly.

Eileen was the first one to ask Mr. Taylor what kind of business he was planning to start.

Penelope interjected, "Maybe we should wait for Mr. Taylor himself to tell us, when he's ready."

"I have no objection at all," said Richard, with a bright smile on his face. "I'm going to start an import/export business to bring to Victoria wares from all over the world. I have contacts in India, Iran, China, Europe as well as South America."

"That is wonderful," said Eileen. "I look forward to visiting your store. By the way where is it going to be?"

"I'm very sorry but I forgot to mention that my business will be a wholesale business. I'll be the supplier to different stores on the Island, and will only have a small warehouse. But, for all of you people, I'll make an exception. Once I'm fully stocked, anyone of you can visit me at the warehouse to buy for yourselves at a reduced price. Now, I would be grateful if you didn't spread the word around. I certainly wouldn't want to offend any of my future store buyers."

Penelope became aware that once again she was daydreaming about the new boarder. Felicity coming in with the platters for the table brought her back to reality. She stood up and told everyone that she had an announcement to make and would Felicity stay with her for a moment.

All eyes, some puzzled, were staring at her. Everyone was very attentive wanting to hear as soon as possible what was so important.

"I would like all of you to know that, if at anytime, more so at night, you have an urge for a snack before going to bed, please let Felicity know after dinner. She'll be more than pleased to prepare some small snack for you. All of you are free to wander anywhere on these premises except for the kitchen. I hope that this offends none of you. Because we have to prepare our menu ahead of time, it can be very disturbing, if not aggravating for the chef when she's looking for a certain item and finds it missing. Is everyone comfortable with that?"

They all agreed. The conversation picked up where it had stopped. Joyce was glad for that and kept quiet.

Penelope had a hard time avoiding looking at her new boarder. Even in his demeanor Richard Taylor reminded her of Jason McKee. She was starting to have second thoughts about Mr. Taylor being part of the boarding house, not that he wasn't a gentleman and all that, but because it raised in her, feelings that had been dormant for some time and that made her uneasy. She was hoping no one else would notice her disquiet especially Joyce, who had a big mouth. Miss Mahoney freely spoke her mind regardless of the consequences.

They all started to get up to wish each other good night which left Penelope alone, deep in thought. Immediately Felicity came back into the dining room to clean up the table.

"My oh! My," said Felicity, "are we in dreamland tonight or is there something bothering you, my dear lady?"

Penelope was startled by the voice and answered, "No not at all, I was just thinking ahead. Wondering how many more boarders we should accept." *What an excuse, she thought.* "We are seven at this time, including you, Sam and I, do you think we could take on three more boarders or would that be too much work?"

"First, my dear Penelope," said Felicity. "I want to thank you for your little speech tonight.

I'm sure the guilty party got the message and will follow the rules. Secondly, tomorrow morning Nanette is coming over. I would like you to meet her. She's the one who will be my 'marmiton.' She's only twenty-one but a very hard worker. More importantly, she wants to learn how to cook and serve. I agreed that I would show her. You can pay her $8.00 a day, which I think, will make her happy. As I told you before, she lives with her mother around the corner from here. Her father is in the Navy; he's out at sea a lot. She'll only have lunch, possibly dinner as well, with me, in the kitchen. One more mouth to feed will not cost a penny extra. Is that agreeable with you?"

"I think I would like to pay her thirty dollars a week in the beginning," said Penelope. "If it turns out that she's a big help to you, at a later time, we can make other arrangements. Right now until we have a full house, I would prefer this arrangement better. What do you think?"

"I'm sure she'll agree," said Felicity. "She did finish grade twelve but does not have a university degree. As she has no office experience, she can't find work with the provincial government or any secretarial jobs anywhere. Besides, she's a very bubbly person with an easy smile and she loves to be in the kitchen preparing food. When she gets here tomorrow morning, sometime after breakfast, I'll introduce her so you can judge for yourself."

On that note, Felicity left the dining room and Penelope decided to go watch some television in the library.

As she walked in, she noticed that one chair was occupied, the television was on, so she figured that her brother was watching. "Well, Sam, what are you watching tonight?" she asked.

To her surprise, the voice that came back to her in the semi-darkness was different from her brother's. She quickly realized it wasn't Sam!

"Oh! Mr. Taylor, I didn't mean to startle you," she exclaimed! "I'm sorry I interrupted your concentration."

"Not at all Mrs. Woodspring, I was just killing time basically putting my thoughts together, thinking about my business dealings tomorrow."

"By the way, Mr. Taylor, for the record, it is Miss Woodspring. Please keep on watching your program. As I told the guests at dinner, you have access to all the 'public' rooms in this old house. All I ask is that the last person leaving, kindly turn off the television as well as the lights."

"You're too kind, Miss Woodspring, if you don't mind my saying so. You're not disturbing me at all. I have the Ed Sullivan Show on. As you can see, one does not have to think too much, and it fills in the hour. Would you like to watch with me or did you have some other program in mind? CBC may have something good on tonight!"

"Whatever's on, is fine with me," Penelope said. "I'm pleased that you had the opportunity to meet the other guests tonight. We certainly have a diverse group as you've probably noticed."

"They appear to be all very nice people. That Eileen is quite a spunky little lady. She reminds me of an old aunt of mine from back east. Quite a lively person I must say," he added! "Is Mr. Van Orsdal a retired professor?"

"You know, Richard...sorry, I mean Mr. Taylor," she corrected herself, "I really don't know the background of all my guests, Van Orsdal is one that I would like to find out about. He must have had quite an interesting life."

"You can call me Richard, it's quite all right. I would feel better if you did. Mr. Taylor sounds so official, after all, as you said, we are like a family, are we not?"

"Thank you," she answered, "and on that I must bid you goodnight as I have a busy day tomorrow."

Penelope got up quickly to leave. She was grateful for the semi-darkness as she felt her cheeks blushing a bit, for some reason being alone around that man did something to her. *My God,* she thought, *I feel like a schoolgirl who has a crush on the teacher. I had better go to bed, have a good rest to regain my composure. Oh well, tomorrow is another day.* She felt herself smiling in the darkness.

She wondered how it would be to have a new lover! "What am I thinking about?" she said to herself. "This man is a paying guest in my boarding house. I'll just have to control my emotions when Richard Taylor is around. But it feels good to know I'm still alive."

The following day, Penelope was up bright and early. As she walked into the dining room, found herself alone again with Richard, she greeted him "good morning" sat down for coffee just as Eileen walked in with her cheerful happy face.

"How is everybody today?" she chanted with a smile.

Richard took the moment to mention to Penelope how he admired the beautiful Gaugin hanging on the wall above the Georgian buffet.

"I acquired that drawing when on a trip to Tahiti some years back," Penelope said. "I do have a few more paintings and drawings from my world travels that I will eventually hang on the walls." The other guests came in which gave Penelope the excuse she needed to leave for the kitchen where she wanted to talk with Felicity.

As she entered, she saw a young lady in her early twenties standing near the working area listening to Felicity's instructions.

Felicity introduced her to Penelope as Nanette Marchand whom she had hired to be her "marmiton."

Penelope was pleased to meet her. She immediately realized how pretty as well as pleasant this young woman was. "I hope you enjoy being part of our big family Nanette," she said. "I'm sure that Felicity will show you around to help you familiarize yourself with this old house."

"Thank you, Madame," said Nanette in her very cute French accent. "I am certain that I will learn very much from Miss Felicity."

Penelope inquired of Felicity if there was anything she needed for the kitchen or otherwise.

"Not at this time, my dear lady, everything is under control. I don't think any shopping is needed until tomorrow."

Penelope left to go to the library where her desk was set up, picked up the telephone to call Edward, the handyman, as some cleaning up around the garden was needed before the winter settled in. A tremendous amount of leaves had covered the front lawn as well as the back garden. Edward assured her that he would be there within a couple of days to clean it up, but before hanging up he inquired if Miss Flowers was still living there, wondering how she was.

Penelope assured him she was fine, telling him she would relay his concern along with his wishes to the lady.

Just as she was getting up from her desk, she noticed a small envelope placed on its edge at the far left, almost hidden behind the telephone. It must have dropped there somehow. It was addressed to her. It certainly aroused her curiosity, she wondered who would have left it there and why. She picked up her old-fashioned wooden letter opener, which she had bought during a trip to South Africa with Jason, and opened the envelope. She started to read the note inside which she found to be an invitation to High Tea at the Empress Hotel for the following Sunday, signed by Richard Taylor.

"How lovely," she said. "Sunday Tea at the Empress, I have a feeling that this man is trying to make a date with me." *Well,* she thought, *isn't that interesting!*

After sitting there thinking for some time, she said out loud, "Why not," just as Sam walked into the library.

"What is going on, my dear sister, you seem to have regained your happy disposition. Is it good news from somewhere? You can tell me, you know."

"No, Sam," she said half-laughing, "it is none of your business and yes I do feel a bit better now that we're getting more boarders." She went on more seriously; "Edward is going to come by either today or tomorrow to clean up the leaves from around the property. Would you make sure, my dear brother, that there are enough containers or bags that he can use? Maybe when you go to the market with Felicity you could buy some."

Sam thought to himself that something or someone had to be the cause of his sister's sudden upsurge of enthusiasm. *I wonder if it has anything to do with this new boarder? For some reason he reminds me of someone I know, but I just can't put my finger on who it is! Oh, well she's old enough to know what she's doing, I hope.*

As Sam entered the kitchen he saw this good-looking young woman standing over the worktable. Just as he was going to say something, Felicity called him and said; "Sam this is Nanette, my new helper, she lives around the corner from here. From today on you'll be seeing a lot of her around this kitchen."

"Pleased to meet you, Nanette, I'm Penelope's brother, handyman around the house as well as gofer extraordinaire."

"I am very pleased to meet you, Monsieur Sam. Where do you play golf?" said Nanette.

"I didn't mean golfer, Nanette," he said with a smile, "I said 'gofer,' you know; doing errands, going here, there everywhere."

Felicity interrupted by saying; "Nanette, Sam is our Jack of all Trades. When we need supplies from the market, he'll drive us there. You're here just in time, Sam. A moment ago I realized I need to get some supplies from the market. Later this morning, would you be kind enough to take us there?"

"Anytime you're ready, just give me the word," he said as he left the kitchen area wishing that he were twenty years younger!

If only Eileen Flowers would not make those "goo-goo" eyes at him in front of the others he would certainly not be so uncomfortable around her, he thought. There has to be a way to divert her interest towards someone else, either old Van Orsdal or maybe Edward the handyman. *Well, here's a thought that might just do the trick.* Sam remembered that Edward did have an eye for the old girl. He would have to work on that one.

***

Late autumns are always beautiful in Victoria, a bit of sunshine, a bit of rain, cooler than the summer days but still lots of greenery around.

It seemed that some of the leaves stayed on the trees forever.

Penelope was taking a walk around the property early on Saturday morning, just looking to see if there was any major work to be done before the rainy winter months came along. She suddenly heard a familiar voice from behind her; "Looking for something to do or are you just admiring the beauty of this old mansion?"

"Well, good morning, Richard," blurted Penelope. "I did not expect to meet anyone out here this early in the morning. By the way, I got your invitation for Sunday. I'll be pleased to join you for High Tea at the Empress. It'll do me good to get away from this house, if only for a few hours. I haven't had a chance to be away from here in the past few months with all the renovations and repairs going on. Had to keep an eye on things, you know."

"I'm glad that you accept my invitation Penelope," said Richard with a smile. "I look forward to a beautiful tomorrow. Shall we say at 2.30 PM or is another time more convenient for you?"

"Two-thirty will be fine Richard," she said as he walked over to the old mansion for breakfast.

***

Everyone appeared to be cheerful at breakfast except for Reginald Van Orsdal who was behaving like a lion in a cage.

Joyce made the comment that he looked like an old tomcat that had spent the night roaming the back alleys!

"I'll have you know, my dear lady, if I can call you that," snorted Van Orsdal, "I'm not a night watchman, if that's what you mean. Besides, I'd like you to mind your own business."

"My oh! My, we are a little snippy this morning," said Eileen, as she looked at Sam with her big bedroom-eyes including a big grin on her face. They could always count on Eileen to be perky, smiling and generally happy. She had that kind of disposition, not an ounce of meanness in her, always happy-go-lucky!

Sam thought that if he intervened, it would break the tension so he said, "I'm going to the market this morning. Does anyone need anything? If you do, just give me your list after breakfast. I'll be happy to oblige."

***

Penelope had accepted Richard Taylor's invitation to High Tea without hesitation. Yet, something was telling her to be cautious. Was she walking into a nightmare? Time would tell.

CHAPTER NINE

Fall had arrived along with the cold weather; the winds as well as the rain had come too soon for Penelope. It had been three weeks now since she had enjoyed that wonderful afternoon at the Empress with Richard. She had found out from him that he was a widower with no children, had moved here from a suburb of Toronto to avoid the winter climate as well as the fast city life.

That is what he had told her. She felt comfortable with it for now. Penelope figured that was enough information for the time being. Prying into one's personal affairs was not her style.

Late November was miserable weatherwise in Victoria. The stores had already started to advertise the Christmas Season. For some reason, the lights and decorations lacked the cheeriness of other Canadian cities, perhaps due to the lack of snow. There were office Christmas parties happening all over the place, the downtown restaurants were buzzing with people in a cheerful holiday mood.

At the boarding house Penelope had asked Edward and Sam to put up some lights around the front of the old mansion.

It gave it an air of festivity in the winter darkness. Edward had suggested waiting until about mid-December before putting up a Christmas tree in the parlor.

Eileen and Joyce were leaving in early December to spend the holiday season with relatives in other parts of the country. Mr. Van Orsdal mentioned that he would certainly enjoy the peace as well as the quiet that the departure of Miss Mahoney, for however short of a time, would bring to the place.

Penelope did not want to plan any special event for the Holiday Season. In past years she would have been somewhere in the world where the climate was milder but this year she decided to stay in Victoria.

***

One morning as she was stepping out for her early morning stroll around the property, she noticed a huge white Cadillac pulling into the driveway. Someone must have the wrong address, she thought, as she approached the car. She noticed that the driver was the most strikingly beautiful woman she had seen in a long time. As the lady gracefully stepped out of the car, Penelope saw that she must be in her early forties. She was dressed elegantly with the look of ageless beauty a few very rich women and movie stars have; with plenty of money to spend on their appearance it made it easier. Her only make-up was a pale pink lipstick so transparent it served only to accent the true color of her full lips. No lines or wrinkles marred her looks.

"May I help you?" asked Penelope.

"My name is Hanna Mueller," the stranger said in a cultured voice. "I'm an avid student of Victorian-era architecture. I could not resist stopping for a moment to admire this lovely home. Are you the owner?"

"Yes I am. My name is Penelope Woodspring. What brings you to our part of the world? I notice that you have American plates on your car. Are you just visiting?"

"I decided to take time off. Drive to Victoria for a visit since I had not been here before," Mueller said. "Would you believe that I made a wrong turn on my way to the hotel. When I saw your beautiful home, I could not resist the temptation to stop and have a look! I hope you don't mind my boldness!"

"Not at all," answered Penelope "you're welcome to look at the inside with me, if you wish. Are you in Victoria for long?"

"I'm going to be here for a couple of weeks. Just enough time to refresh myself as well as restoring my energy for when I get back to the grind of doing a television series. I play the leading role in this new series called 'The Spy', it's on NBC Thursday nights. It's about a rich socialite who gets tangled up with a CIA agent. She's asked to help her country to uncover some criminal elements that have infiltrated North America from Eastern Europe. Have you seen any of it yet?"

"I must admit that I'm not a regular television viewer," said Penelope. "I would rather sit and read a good book. But now that you've told me about it, I'll certainly look for your show next week. By the way, Miss Mueller, would you like to have coffee with us in the dining room, I think that as a person with interest in Victorian styles, you'll find it quite unusual."

As they entered the house, Hanna was struck by the decor of its walls and ceilings. They entered the dining room where they were met by Felicity. After the introductions were made, Felicity served a cup of coffee with fresh-baked muffins. "These muffins are delicious," said Miss Mueller. "Where did you get them?"

"I bake them myself," said Felicity proudly.

***

After coffee and muffins, Penelope took her new-found television star for a grand tour of the old house.

"You certainly have a beautiful home Miss Woodspring. I can't thank you enough for showing me around," Hanna enthused.

"Maybe on your next vacation you can spend some time with us if you would like," ventured Penelope. "This is run as a boarding house. Our rates are very reasonable."

"You know my dear lady," answered Hanna, "you have just given me a thought. As you have some spare rooms, would you rent me one for a two-week period?"

"I can certainly do that, but what about your hotel reservation?" said Penelope.

"If I can use your telephone I'll just call and cancel it. How much will you charge me?" asked Hanna.

Penelope did some fast figuring and told her that for a two-week period, including all meals with a change of linen twice a week it would be $300.00. "Is that acceptable to you?"

"Of course it is," replied Hanna. "The hotel alone was going to cost me more."

They went together to the library where Penelope's work desk was. Miss Mueller sat down, took out a notebook from her purse to check the telephone number and dialed the hotel.

After Hanna hung up with the hotel Penelope asked her if she was sure she'd rather stay at the boarding house.

"Miss Woodspring, after seeing your place, meeting your chef, I wouldn't want to stay anywhere else," said Hanna.

She took her wallet from her purse, counted a full $300.00 and handed it to Penelope. "Here, that should take care of my stay. Do you have someone who could take my luggage in?"

"Certainly, my brother Sam will. But first let me show you the room that I have in mind for you," she said as they went up to the third floor of the Old house.

The room was large with a queen-size canopy bed, and its own bathroom with an old style freestanding bathtub. The view from the large bay window gave one a panoramic view of Victoria Harbor, the Legislative Buildings as well as a corner view of the Empress Hotel.

"This is very beautiful, Miss Woodspring, I'm sure I'll have a peaceful stay. No crowds like you always have in hotels. What a lucky find for me," Hanna added.

***

Early December saw an increase in activity at the boarding house. Eileen and Joyce were both preparing to go on their separate trips. Richard Taylor was busy with preparations at his warehouse on the Gorge. With the help of Sam, Edward had put up all the Christmas decorations in addition to the colored lights. It made the old mansion look like a picture out of a child's fairy tale book, certainly brightening up Military Street.

Hanna Mueller was spending a lot of time playing the tourist game. First to Butchart Gardens, then the downtown Museum. Next were all the art galleries especially those with Indian art done by local as well as British Columbia artists. During her second week, Hanna asked Penelope if her brother Sam would mind driving her around town, as she wanted to get to know Victoria better.

"I don't think Sam will mind at all! As a matter of fact I think that he'll be happy to drive you around. Cars have always been a hobby of his. I've caught him many times eyeing your Cadillac with an envious look on his face."

***

What the people in the boarding house didn't know was the true identity of Hanna Mueller. She was an undercover agent for the FBI

investigating drug smuggling from British Colum-
bia, more specifically from the Vancouver Island
area. Her cover-up as a television actress was re-
markable because there really was such a person
by that name playing a leading role in an NBC
Spy type series. Hanna was made up to resemble
the actress to protect her own identity.

***

The FBI had received a tip from an informer that a major drug smuggling operation was
being set-up somewhere in BC. They had obtained
the co-operation of the Royal Canadian Mounted
Police to have their own agent handle the investigation.

The head of this smuggling group was a
Benjamin Malouf also known under several alias-
es, including Richard Taylor. He was a master
forger, a con man extraordinaire whose mother
tongue was Spanish. Taylor spoke several other
languages including English as well as French.
What was so exceptional about his ability to speak
these languages fluently, is that he did it without a
trace of any foreign accent.

Hanna was looking at a city map while
Sam was slowly cruising towards downtown. She
asked him to drive to an area called the Gorge Waterway.

Sam was ecstatic about driving the big
Cadillac with such a beautiful lady beside him.

At one point, she asked him to stop to have
a closer look at the magnificent view. Stepping out
of the car with camera in hand, like any good tour-

ist, she appeared to be taking snap shots of the area. What she was really doing was taking pictures of the construction of a small warehouse with access to a docking facility. She knew that this was the place where Malouf would store his imported goods. She wanted to make sure that other agents would have a good view of the access as well as possible get-away routes from the warehouse.

As the investigation was only beginning, she would have to come back to the area a few more times to familiarize herself with all the surroundings. She took a few more pictures even asking Sam if he would be kind enough to take a couple of shots of her with the waterway as a background.

Sam was all thumbs but after she showed him how to use the camera he was quite happy to oblige her.

Imagine, he thought, *me, just little old me, taking a photograph of a famous television star. I must ask her to give me a copy.*

After the pictures were taken, they returned to Military Street. Hanna was very appreciative and wanted to give Sam a tip but he refused. "When you get your film developed, send me one of the pictures that I took of you. That will be my payment," he said with a big smile on his face.

She agreed to do this as she made sure to ask for a boarding house business card.

***

Everyone was cheerful at dinner that night. Eileen happily mentioned that this would be her first trip to visit her daughter in three years. She wanted them all to know that Edward was going along with her.

What no one suspected, except Sam, was that she and Edward had been seeing each other on a regular basis for the past seven weeks or so.

"Being away for three weeks at Christmas time, leaving Edward here alone would not be proper," she said with a smile, looking at Sam.

Joyce said that she looked forward to visiting her two old aunts whom she had not seen in several years. Both Eileen and Joyce were leaving the next morning; they wanted to wish everybody a happy holiday season.

Hanna Mueller took the opportunity to tell them how pleased she was to have met such a good group of people. Furthermore, she appreciated the way they all treated her.

Richard Taylor in his usual well-behaved manner said to everyone that the French wine being served with dinner tonight was his way of showing his appreciation to these wonderful people at the boarding house.

Not to be left out, Reginald Van Orsdal in his best English extended his greetings to everyone wishing the two traveling ladies a safe journey.

Everyone left the dining room except for Penelope and Richard, who were both savoring the last of the wine.

"You know, Penelope, there's a dance in Cordova Bay on Saturday at a restaurant with a ballroom that overlooks the ocean. The view is fantastic. From what I've heard, they always have a good orchestra, the Big Band style of music that we had some years ago. Would you like to go there with me?"

Penelope finished slowly sipping her wine then said, "That is the best invitation I've had since High Tea. I would be honored to shuffle my feet on the dance floor with you but I may step on your toes a few times, as I haven't danced in years."

"I'll wear an old pair of shoes if you don't mind," Richard added with tongue in cheek.

***

The following morning, Sam drove Eileen, Edward and Joyce to the Airport in Miss Mueller's Cadillac. Hanna had insisted, as he would have had to make two trips with old 'Agnes' instead of one with the Cadillac. Hanna went along for the ride as well. She wanted to familiarize herself with the whole area so that she would be able to include details in a report to her superiors upon her return to the United States.

On the way back she asked Sam to drive by the Gorge Waterway again. She wanted to have a look again at the beautiful setting. What she really had in mind was to check up on the construction that was going on at Malouf's.

This Benjamin Malouf was a really smooth operator. His Lebanese father was a worldwide trader; he could not have had a better teacher. The father's connections with the existing French underworld as well as the South American drug cartel, was a fountain of knowledge for young Benjamin. His family history had been well documented by Interpol and the Federal Bureau of Investigation in the United States.

***

Hanna did not think or believe that Penelope was involved in any way whatsoever in Malouf's drug business. He was just using her in addition to the boarding house as a cover-up. Or so he thought.

She really wanted to tell Penelope about this man, to be careful about her relationship with him. But she knew well enough that to put doubt in someone's mind, especially someone as intelligent as Penelope, could blow her own cover along with the whole investigation. There was too much at stake here for her to do that. She would just have to leave it alone and let the chips fall where they may, hoping that being the wonderful person Penelope was, she would not be hurt too badly.

***

That same night at dinner Hanna informed everyone that she would be leaving the following morning. she wanted all of them to know how she had enjoyed her stay at the boarding house. She assured them she would return in springtime to enjoy the entire lovely blossoming trees and flowers for which Victoria was so famous. Looking at

Sam she thanked him for being such a good tourist guide and would he mind taking her luggage down in the morning?

"It will be a pleasure," said Sam. "But I will certainly miss your company."

Penelope interjected saying that Sam would probably miss driving the Cadillac more, causing everyone to have a good chuckle, including her brother.

CHAPTER TEN...

After breakfast on a Friday morning, Richard Taylor drove to Nanaimo to meet two associates from back east who had arrived by ferry from the mainland. They were driving a car with Alberta license plates. He met them in a downtown restaurant crowded enough so as not to attract too much attention.

Gabrielli Vito, usually called "Gabby," was the cousin of the Vitriolli family that controlled the underworld business in the eastern part of Canada. His job was to ensure that the drug business expanded to all parts of Western Canada as well as the northwestern states.

In the scheme of things, Benjamin Malouf was their front man because of his worldwide business contacts with the Columbia drug cartel. He spoke several languages fluently, including Italian.

Giovanni Saturno, known as 'Gino the eliminator,' was Gabby's personal bodyguard, trusted associate; on this trip, he was the driver/observer, sidekick, a very muscular and athletic young man in his late twenties.

When Benji, as they called him, arrived at the designated restaurant in downtown Nanaimo, he was greeted with a big smile and a handshake from Gabby. Gino just nodded his head in recognition. His blue eyes had a steely look, and seemed to bore right through you. He had an ominous air about him. Taylor was glad not to be at odds with this mean-looking young man.

Gabby told him he had received a report on the setting-up of the import/export business and felt really good about it. They were sure that the cover-up was perfect, up to this point anyway. The shipments were to begin arriving in about five or six weeks and would be well camouflaged within each crate of merchandise. He went on to explain that each wooden box would contain about twenty-two to forty identical items. Seventy percent of these items would have an "x" scratched on the bottom. When broken open, a plastic bag containing pure cocaine would fall out. The first shipment would have about 140 of these crates along with another sixty to seventy pieces of furniture. Gabby added it would be followed by a similar shipment two months later.

Richard Taylor was quite impressed at how Gabby had organized the whole process. Getting the suppliers was not the difficult part, especially when you had the cash to pay for it.

What had intrigued Richard was how the drug packets had been hidden within the shipment. He was also informed that a different code would be used each time to let him know where the packets were hidden.

Gabby told him that for safety purposes they had to change the method of packaging on each shipment. He further remarked; "I was thinking that you may want to have someone like Gino with you when the first shipment arrives."

"No offense, Gabby, but so far things have been going in the right direction. I would prefer having my local workers receiving the crates. Besides, I'll be the only one checking the 'merchandise' once it's in my warehouse. I would prefer to have it that way, if you don't mind," said Richard.

"It's OK with me," said Gabby, "but if you ever have a need for 'security' I'll be happy to make Gino available to you. He can be trusted to 'eliminate' any potential problem you may have, *capish*?"

Gabby told Gino to wait for him and Benji in the restaurant, whilst they went for a walk together.

Once outside, Gabby started the conversation by saying that he had not shown up a few weeks ago because they had found a "mole" in one sector of the organization. He believed that this person was responsible for several leaks to the local RCMP in Montreal. Anyhow, the problem had now been eliminated, resting comfortably in a concrete box at the bottom of the St. Lawrence River.

Gabby went on to say that they had been successful in obtaining from this person most of the information he had supplied to the police. Fortunately all he had known about the western operation was that he, Gabby, and an associate were going to Vancouver shortly.

In order to break the trail, Gabby said, he had gone to New Brunswick instead, taken a flight to Halifax, rented a car, drove back to Quebec City and from there took another flight to Toronto. Once there, an acquaintance got him a safe car, and he picked up Gino, who took care of the driving to the West Coast. "One cannot be too careful with this operation," Gabby said. "I believe we're looking at hundreds of millions once this business is functional. This is why you're here, Benji! My uncle would not trust just anybody in such an important venture.

        "We're keeping a close eye on the operation strictly to protect you. Back east we're scrutinizing everyone in our operations who is not 'family'. We can't have the possibility of losing shipment after shipment. Our investment is too great as well as the potential profits too enormous to be treated lightly. I have a briefcase in the car for you, containing money that you'll need to move things around faster when you go to the States. There's $300,000.00 in American cash and $400,000.00 in Canadian money. You may have to do a dry run to Seattle in order to establish contact. Please remember to do all transactions in cash with everyone.

        "That way it stays untraceable," said Gabby. "If you need help in any way you just have to let me know. Don't use your own telephone, go to a pay phone somewhere in town, that way it's impossible to trace. Gino doesn't know what's in the briefcase. I want to keep it that way. Only my Uncle Leonardo, you and I are aware of this whole deal so far!"

"As you know, Gabby, I'm using the name Richard Taylor. All my identification papers are made to that name so that when we're with people, please call me Richard. Otherwise you may slip up causing someone to get suspicious."

"No problem with that, Richard," said Gabby. "We're going to drive back to Calgary and take a flight from there. Just keep me informed on any major changes that occur or might have to be made. This is a big operation, Richard; we can't afford to muck it up! Have you had anyone snooping around, asking questions about your business or problems of any kind since you've been in Victoria?"

"Certainly not any that I could detect," said Richard. "Some weeks ago there was some female actress from California whom I thought could be a plant. I had the plate numbers of her car verified, and they matched her name and where she said she lived. One can never be too careful in our type of business. By the way, try not to call me at my residence unless it's a real emergency. Next weekend I'm going to Seattle with the lady of the house. Oh! Don't worry Gabby, she doesn't suspect a thing. This will just be a look-see kind of short trip to familiarize myself with the surroundings. No official contacts will be made or attempted. As a matter of fact we're going to a theater play, dinner and you know…relaxation. It's good for the soul, you ought to try it sometime, Gabby."

On that final comment they decided to walk back towards the restaurant where Gino was waiting.

After picking-up the "briefcase" Richard said good-bye to his associate walking to where he had left his car. As he got closer to where he had parked, he noticed the driver's side window had been smashed. Glass was all over the pavement in addition to the inside of the car. When he looked in, the radio had been stolen the glove compartment was all torn-up. He immediately went to a telephone booth that he could see near the sidewalk, called the local police to report the incident for insurance purposes.

Once the policeman had completed his report and given him a copy, he went to a local autoglass repair shop to have the window replaced. He would replace the radio in Victoria. He wished that he could have caught the petty thieves. He disliked this kind of behavior. On the other hand was glad he had not left anything of value or even incriminating in the car.

On his way back to Victoria many thoughts went through his mind. First the visit from Gabby Vito, which he knew was coming and necessary for the transfer of cash. *Bank transactions can always be traced,* he thought, *this was a better way of doing it.* Then, meeting Gino with those steely cold eyes that gave him chills up and down his spine. The least he saw of him the better.

Richard thought of Penelope. Yes, poor naïve Penelope who appeared to have no street smarts. Still he must be careful not to do anything that would arouse doubts or suspicions on her part. He wondered if she had a safe in the house where he could keep his cash hidden until he needed it. Well, he would certainly find out.

When he finally arrived in Victoria, it was late afternoon. He went directly to an auto-audio shop to have his car stereo replaced. They told him that he would have to come back in the morning or leave the car with them. He decided to leave the car there and take a taxi home. Tomorrow was Saturday, the right time to do some reading on the coastal layout of Vancouver Island for future adventures.

***

Penelope was busy in the kitchen working with Nanette to help get breakfast on the table for the guests as Felicity had gone away for the weekend. Once she saw that the 'marmiton' had everything under control she went to the dining room to join her guests. As she took her seat, Richard was just finishing telling Reginald Van Orsdal about the car break-in he had been a victim of yesterday.

"What's this I hear about someone being robbed?" Penelope asked.

"Nothing that dangerous," Richard said. "It's just that some vandal broke the window of my car tearing off the radio from the dash. It's more of an aggravation than a cost. I'm having it fixed in town. They assured me it should be ready by noon today. In the meantime I'm just going to relax and forget about it. Besides I had a very busy fruitful day so I can't complain too much."

As breakfast was winding down, Penelope and Richard were left alone. He chose the moment to ask her if she had a secure place for valuables, such as a safe, somewhere in the house? He wanted to put some valuables away without having a safety deposit box at the local bank as he found it to be a nuisance to deal with.

"I sure do. It's a great big safe in the library that you're welcome to use," said Penelope. "Only my brother Sam and I have the combination, if that's not inconvenient for you," Penelope answered.

"Well thank you, that is very kind of you to oblige. I have a briefcase with some valuables in addition to a substantial amount of cash I keep for quick deals when necessary. If I may, I'll bring my briefcase over immediately for safe-keeping," Richard replied.

As Richard left for the guesthouse, Sam returned to the dining room to tell his sister he would not be home for dinner tonight. He was going over to visit with Jennifer Lyle, his newly found friend.

Penelope reminded her brother not to forget to take flowers along with him. "By the way", she said; "Richard Taylor is going to leave a briefcase with some valuables in the safe today. Just so you know since only you and I have the combination."

***

The weekend went by without a hitch. Penelope was pleased to see how efficient Nanette was at preparing the meals. Even though Felicity had organized the menu for her, it still had to be put together with taste.

Sometime on Monday morning, Eileen and Edward returned from their Up Island trip. She told Penelope that it had been years since she experienced such a wonderful time. Besides she said, the scenery is so beautiful.

"We saw some whales far away, I could tell by the water being spouted in the air. Penelope, I want you to be the first to know that we have decided to get married soon. We haven't come up with a definite date yet, but it will be before the summer is over, you can count on that."

Penelope smiled, saying, "Well that is a nice surprise, I'm very happy for you and Edward. Just let me know when I can tell the other 'family' members.

"Not until I give you a date. By the way, do you think that Felicity would accept being my bridesmaid? Do you also think Sam would want to serve as best man for Edward?" inquired Eileen.

"You could not have made a better choice, Eileen, I know they'll both be thrilled."

"I also thought of asking Joyce to play music for us," said Eileen. "Let's talk about the whole thing in a couple of weeks, I'll know by then when my daughter is able to come here," added the bubbly boarder.

***

Later Penelope was just going through some paper work thinking about the up-coming weekend, when the telephone rang. She was surprised to hear Hanna Mueller's voice calling from Southern California. Miss Mueller was inquiring if she could reserve a room for the whole month of July. Would there be the possibility of having an extra room for a friend who was also thinking of coming up to Victoria!

Penelope assured her it was not a problem for her to get a room but she would appreciate knowing shortly about her friend, if that was OK with her.

Hanna told her she would be flying to Victoria this time around, most likely would be renting a car at the airport. She was looking forward to arriving on July 1. Hanna would let her know within a few days what her friend had decided.

***

In the meantime, the on-going police undercover watch placed on Benjamin Malouf was not noticing any activities of drug shipments at the infamous warehouse on the Gorge. For whatever reasons the drug dealers were not moving about.

They wondered if the main character (Richard) had sniffed them out or was just being extra careful. Could it be coincidence that "things" were not happening at this particular time? Was it possible that information supplied by the informants was not accurate? Furthermore, their number one informer had disappeared a few weeks ago without a trace. The investigators found that to be worrisome. It was highly unusual for known criminals to completely cover their tracks without a trace, especially when they were paid informants. Something was not right with the disappearance of a key player. The problem would have to be solved before any major move was made.

Furthermore, the people at headquarters were also concerned about a two-week loss of Gabby Vito's trail. Then he (Vito) showed up at a restaurant in Toronto's little Italy. His sidekick-bodyguard Gino Saturno also reappeared at the same time and place. The top echelon was worried that their main informer, a fellow by the name of Laurent Lemay may have met with foul play.

If that were the case, it would cause some communication problems for some time. It had been and would still be very difficult to penetrate the "inner circle" of the Vitriolli crime family again.

Inspector Hector Lesage of the Royal Canadian Mounted Police (RCMP) in Ottawa was a bit concerned about the whole investigation from the Canadian side of the border. In that respect, he solicited his friendly contacts in Washington DC. A meeting was arranged between them to take place in Los Angeles. At this meeting it was decided to send Hanna Mueller (better known as Special Agent Joan Brent) back to Victoria, British Columbia. In addition to agent Brent, another female agent would be sent to more closely watch Benjamin Malouf's activities. Malouf was the main player in this international scheme.

Co-operation was very important between the two police forces since the American agents were least likely to be known or recognized by the Canadian gangsters. The decision was quickly made. Action had to be taken without compromising the concept. Malouf and his contacts in the Middle East were not the easiest people to catch. They were well organized. Anyone who was involved with them knew the consequences of breaking the "law of silence". Death without pity, in many instances, torture as well as dismemberment to deter others.

Inspector Lesage was a bit apprehensive about sending the same agent who had been there before! Was her cover good enough to withstand scrutiny? They must never underestimate those "Mafiosos". If they had any kind of suspicion about someone, they had their own way of checking it out before eliminating the problem.

His American counterpart assured him that the covers given first to Special Agent Brent and to her colleague had been tested thoroughly. Both covers appeared to be 100% leak-proof.

They all decided to be careful, just simply do some surveillance, watching the activities from a distance so as not to arouse suspicion. Furthermore, their Middle Eastern agents would be contacted to find out what activities were going on in their area. It seemed unusual to the investigators that no information whatsoever had been gathered on possible drugs shipments to North America.

"Perhaps its the quiet before the storm," speculated the Inspector. "Should that be the case, we have to keep track of all the players involved on both sides of the border. As you know gentlemen, we have not been able to locate our number one informer in Montreal. Almost three weeks ago Laurent Lemay disappeared from the face of the earth. Not a trace to follow that could have helped us locate him. This leads us to believe that somehow he was discovered by the 'family' and disposed of somewhere."

"Their usual procedure is the use of concrete to prevent any findings, but the question is where is the body if a body there is to be found? They often torture police informers in order to get information from them about what they may have told the cops. If this is the case, then the New York as well as the Montreal crime syndicate is aware that we're watching them. That is probably why the operation has been rather quiet in the past weeks," said Inspector Lesage. "I'm sure that because of the tremendous amount of money involved, they'll not be inactive too long. But as we all know gentlemen, we cannot afford to make a mistake ourselves, so let's keep this operation of ours as low profile as can be done to avoid detection."

All parties agreed that one mistake would blow the undercover surveillance and besides, it was too early in the scheme of things to fully expose this smuggling group.

CHAPTER ELEVEN...

The holiday season went by without any problems of note at the boarding house on Military Street.

Twice Penelope had been out dancing with Richard Taylor, both times in beautiful Cordova Bay. The restaurant is like an oasis way out in the country. Yet it was only twenty minutes from town driving in Richard's powerful motor car. She had had a very good time with him, especially in December when the Big Band was playing. He had not made any approaches to get intimate with her, not that she minded but it made her wonder if there could be something physically wrong with him.

"No," she said to herself, "it's probably too soon after the death of his wife." At times he appeared to be pre-occupied. Especially when they were out together she caught him off guard a few times when he seemed to be distracted.

He excused himself for being absent minded; saying that starting up a business just kept him very pre-occupied. What he did not tell her was that he was expecting a shipment of plaster statuettes as well as other ornaments from South America. To him these items were very special as they contained pure cocaine. For his own safety he had to make sure the packaging had been done properly. Richard also had to arrange somehow to bring a quantity of packages across the border in Seattle for the American market where the demand was much greater.

***

It was already mid-January when Joyce Mahoney returned to Victoria. She had so much to tell about her old aunts that a couple of evenings were necessary to tell it all. Even Reginald Van Orsdal was attentive as he realized that Joyce was a really good storyteller. Not to mention that he enjoyed not having to see or hear her on a daily basis for the past month!

The following week Eileen returned with Edward in tow. They had the looks of newlyweds, especially Eileen who was quick to tell everyone about their wonderful trip. She told how her children as well as her grandchildren had taken to Edward. No, there were no wedding bells in sight, they were just happy to be back with everyone again.

Penelope welcomed them back as she informed Edward that a few things were there for him to look after as Sam was leaving in a day or two on a business trip to Calgary.

***

One morning in early February as Penelope was finishing her second cup of coffee, she heard the chimes of the front door bell, got up to answer it but Felicity was quicker than she.

When the door opened this tall, well-dressed, not yet middle-aged woman stood there with a smile on her face.

She said good morning and inquired if there were any rooms available.

"Come on in," said Felicity, "the owner is right here and she'll help you."

"My name is Margot Helmsway," the visitor said. "I've just arrived from Montreal. The taxi driver brought me here when I asked him if he knew of a good boarding house where one could stay for a week or two."

Penelope smiled saying, "I'm Penelope Woodspring. I'll be happy to show you what we have available at this time. I hope that you don't mind walking up the stairs. Would you please follow me?"

When they arrived on the third floor, Penelope took her visitor immediately to the room that had previously been occupied by Hanna Mueller.

Margot just loved the antique furniture as well as the magnificent view. She turned to Penelope inquiring, "How much would this be for four weeks?"

Penelope did some quick figuring then said, "Including three meals a day it will cost you one hundred and fifty dollars a week, if this meets your expectations, Miss Helmsway?"

"That really sounds good to me," said Margot as she searched in her purse, for her wallet. "I hope that you don't mind me giving you cash Miss Woodspring? Here's six hundred dollars for the four weeks."

Penelope took the money, thanked her and gave her an overview of the house rules. "When we get back downstairs, I'll get my handyman Edward to help you with your luggage," she said.

***

Margot Helmsway was introduced to the "family" at dinnertime. She explained that she had taken a three-month leave of absence from her job so that she could try to finish the book she had been writing about political scandals in Eastern Canada, especially in Quebec where the Duplessis supporters were at odds. "For that," she said, "I need to be far away from the action in a peaceful environment. Victoria, she had been told, would certainly be the perfect place. So far," she said, "it looks like I've made the right choice."

Eileen in her usual outspoken way asked bluntly, "When do you think we will be able to buy this book of yours? It sounds very mysterious to me. I've always liked mysteries but this is the first time that I have the opportunity to meet an author. I must say that I'm honored to meet you."

"Well," said Margot, "you'll probably see my book in the stores by late next fall."

"That sounds great," said Richard Taylor. "We're very fortunate to have such beautiful as well as talented ladies in this boarding house. Miss Woodspring is here permanently, I'm thankful for that. We also have had a Miss Mueller who's a television star from Hollywood. She was here for a couple of weeks. There's also Miss Felicity, who has delighted our palates on numerous occasions."

Penelope was thankful that no one noticed her blushing cheeks in the candlelight. Richard added, "We must not forget our very talented Miss Mahoney who can entertain us in a most professional way."

"Well thank you for noticing," Joyce said, coyly!

"As you all know why I'm here, I wouldn't mind knowing what you all do," said Margot.

Eileen was the first one to speak. In her own way she said that she was just enjoying life as much as she could. No one knew at this point that Miss Flowers was a rich widow.

"How about you, Mr. Taylor? Are you retired?" asked Margot.

"Not at all Miss Helmsway, I'm in the process of setting up a new business. It's going to be a wholesale import/export venture for which I'm having a warehouse built. As a matter of fact, I'm expecting that I'll be able to begin operations in about four to five weeks," said Richard.

Reginald Van Orsdal just wanted all of them to know that after teaching drama as well as English Literature for over twenty-five years, he was taking a well-needed break. "The University environment is not what it used to be," he said. "The students are not as respectful of the professors as they used to be in my younger days. The time was right for me to get away from it all. I'm also thinking about putting together a theater group here in Victoria, if I can find the right talents."

Joyce invited everyone to the parlor after dinner to give a sample of her entertaining talents.

All in all, it was a lovely evening to remember on that February night at the boarding house on Military Street.

In Penelope's mind, the family atmosphere that she had wanted to create was becoming apparent.

***

Upstairs Margot Helmsway was unpacking her bags, taking out her camera, and setting up her portable typewriter very carefully on the beautiful antique table by the window. Margot thought that her first day in the boarding house had been rather edifying. Who Margot Helmsway really was, she hoped to keep a secret. Federal undercover agents always have to be very prudent so as not to divulge their true purpose or identity.

Her name was real and a cover had been arranged with a Westmount (suburb of Montreal) firm operated by the Federal Customs people. She had been sent to Victoria to check up on Benjamin Malouf, alias Richard Taylor. She'd also been informed that a couple of known underworld characters had left Montreal for Victoria, by road, on the same day that she arrived in Victoria. Her informants had never failed her yet! As she was not known by any of the underworld figures in Montreal, her superiors thought that, rather than a man, she would be better suited for the job of tracking the criminals.

The latter part of February arrived with showers along with warmer weather. Victoria's climate could not be compared to the rest of Canada. The very cold winds and snowstorms of the Western plains as well as the rest of the country's climate rarely reached "La! La! Land," as the Easterners like to call this part of Canada.

Sam returned from his month long trip to Calgary where he had to appear before the Compensation Board to finalize his disability pension. The settlement process was slow so he took the time to visit some friends and of course, invite them to Victoria. He was sure that his sister would not mind them visiting as these people were childhood friends.

Sam had the opportunity of meeting Miss Helmsway at dinner one evening and was informed of her apparent reasons for being in Victoria.

In his usual friendly way, knowing that Penelope would not mind at all, Sam offered to give the new boarder a tour of the greater Victoria area.

She accepted, almost too quickly, then stopped, saying that she would be pleased to take him up on his offer in a day or two.

The guests had left the dining room except for Richard who was finishing a glass of wine. Penelope enjoyed the time when she was left alone with Taylor.

Richard started the conversation by saying that he would need to have a telephone installed in his suite, as he called it. Would she mind supervising the telephone company people when they came to do the installation.

"Well of course not, Richard, Penelope said. "Just tell me when they're supposed to be here. I'll make sure that it's done."

He went on to say that he was intending to take a drive up Island to Nanaimo, possibly a bit further this coming weekend. Would she like to get away from her chores for a day?

"That sounds very inviting," she answered. "I know that you're going there with business in mind. You're sure that I won't be in the way?"

"The business part of the trip will be very short anyway, it can be combined with pleasure, don't you think?" he asked with a smile.

"Well, if you say so, I just didn't want to interfere with any business contacts you may have," she replied.

"Not at all my dear Penelope, I'll look forward to having your company away from Victoria."

She had a hard time hiding her enthusiasm. She certainly didn't want to appear overly anxious. The dim lighting of the dining room was a great help.

***

Early on Saturday morning, Penelope and Richard left for a drive up Island. She had asked

Felicity to make sure that all went well for the weekend. Sam was also asked to keep an eye on the place.

From her upper floor window, Margot saw them leave wondering where they were going. As well, she wanted to find out if anyone else was or was not involved with Benjamin Malouf. From the briefings prior to leaving Montreal, Margot was aware how dangerous this individual known to all as Richard Taylor, could be.

At breakfast Sam was very quiet. He was thinking about his sister and this new boarder. It startled him when Margot walked in.

"I'll take you up on your offer today, if it's all right with you, Sam!"

"That'll be just great," he answered. "I hope that you don't mind riding in old Agnes! From the inside, the color is not bad, besides she purrs along rather well. I'm a fairly good mechanic. I make sure that our car is always in tiptop shape. Did you have any specific area you wanted to see or did you just want to leave it to me?"

"Wherever you wish to take me is fine," said Margot. "I'm sure you're a very good 'cicerone'."

"Well, let's get going then, I'm ready if you are," he said.

***

On that beautiful morning Richard and Penelope had stopped in Duncan for a second cup of coffee. He was unusually talkative. He said that if she didn't mind he would like to go a bit further than Nanaimo. "I hear that Parksville is an up and coming, growing place. But the town I really want to see is called Tofino. I've been told there are beautiful beaches from which you can do whale watching right from the shore. Does that sound interesting to you?" he ventured.

"Of course it does, she said. "You probably know that I haven't been beyond the boundaries of Victoria since we moved here last year. Getting the boarding house ready just kept me too busy to go anywhere. Besides, I don't like to travel by myself. I feel comfortable being with you."

Richard said that he was pleased Penelope enjoyed his company. He commented that likewise, he enjoyed her company.

After finishing the coffee they drove on towards Nanaimo where Richard had decided to stop briefly; he just wanted to find the access to the ferries for future reference. His real interest was to visit Parksville in addition to Tofino with its docking facilities to the Pacific Ocean.

***

At the same time back in Victoria, Sam took Miss Helmsway for a drive around the city. He first went to the beautiful harbor where she took a few snapshots. The Legislative buildings followed where they were able to get a full inside tour, as the government was not yet in session.

Sam then drove to Oak Bay Marina before returning to the city. Margot kept the conversation going by asking Sam if Richard Taylor was his sister's regular boyfriend.

"Why would you ask that?" queried Sam.

"I saw them leave together this morning. I just thought they were close friends," she said.

"Not that I know of," said Sam. "You see, Miss Helmsway, my sister lost her long-time companion several months ago. It has been tough on her, fixing the old house to sell it, then deciding to make a boarding house out of it, at least for the time being. Having a friend, besides her brother, is what I think she needs most at this time."

"By the way, please call me Margot. I was not trying to pry in her personal life; after all, it's none of my business," Margot said apologetically.

So, she thought, Malouf being the con-artist she knew him to be was taking advantage of the situation for his own cover-up. She would have to keep an eye on his (Malouf's) comings and goings to see whom else might be directly involved in his drug operation.

Margot had been informed that the FBI had previously sent someone from across the border to check on Malouf, too. She had been told this agent had stayed at the Boarding House. She supposed there would be a time at some point when all agencies involved in this international operation would compare notes. *Otherwise*, she thought, *we'll certainly trip over one another's feet*.

Sam decided to take her on a tour of the Gorge waterway as he had done with the gorgeous Miss Mueller. As they drove along he pointed out places of interest to her. Suddenly he stopped, parked the car as he invited her to get out too.

He pointed to a construction site near the water. "This is where Richard Taylor is building his warehouse for his import business."

"That's interesting," she said. "I wonder what's being added in front of the building?"

"I think it's a dock," Sam said. "He'll need it as most of his merchandise will be arriving in small ships from different parts of the world, so he once told us."

Margot made a mental note of the area so that she could return on her own to take photographs later.

As soft drizzle had started to come down, they quickly got back into the car for their return to the boarding house.

Driving down Military Street, Margot noticed a car slowly going by the boarding house. Sam mentioned that it might be people admiring the architectural beauty of the old house again.

Margot saw there were two men in the car. She quickly made a mental note of the license plate as well as the make of the vehicle.

"Here we are," said Sam. "Hope you don't get too wet going in. The rain never seems to end, but look at how green everything is, did you ever see so many blooms in February?"

***

On the way north from Duncan, it had started to drizzle. It progressively turned to steady rain as Penelope and Richard arrived in Nanaimo. Water was gushing down the streets like a running creek. They briefly visited the Ferry Terminal then set out for Parksville where, Richard said, they would stop for lunch.

"I thought you wanted to see some business people in Nanaimo, Richard," said Penelope. "Don't let me stop you, I can either wait in the car or in a restaurant if you wish."

"No need to do that, Penelope," Richard said smiling back. "I'm not seeing anyone here today. This trip is just exploratory besides; it was only an excuse to get you to come with me. I hope you are not angry?"

"Not at all," she said. "Quite the contrary, it's a rather good feeling to be with a companion on one's own terms."

When they arrived in Parksville, they chose a restaurant, which had a beautiful view of the ocean. Lunch was going to be a slow affair. Penelope was hoping to get to know this man more than she presently did.

If only Penelope could have seen through this individual for what he really was.

***

It was time for Margot Helmsway to leave Victoria and return to her superiors with a report on what information she had been able to gather. She had taken photographs of the warehouse as well as the site where Malouf had built a dock for his "import/export" business. The one thing bothering her was the two underworld agents who were supposed to make contact with Malouf in Victoria. She had not seen anyone trying to make contact with him. The license number she had jotted down when she had returned from the sight-seeing tour with Sam, turned out to be locals who, as Sam had presumed, were just admiring the old mansion's architecture.

She finished packing her bags, walked down to the library to see Penelope to thank her for the wonderful hospitality. At the same time she asked her to arrange for a taxi to take her to the airport.

***

After Margot's departure, Penelope was sitting at her desk daydreaming about her trip up Island with Richard. He was everything she thought he would be. Gentle, very attentive as well as caring. She had to tell herself not to fall in love. An adventure was fun but no commitments at this time.

If she could only read into the future.

CHAPTER TWELVE...

Reginald Van Orsdal was all set to go ahead about starting his new theatrical training classes. Some weeks ago he had placed an advertisement in the Daily Colonist. The response was greater than he had expected, in all 14 people registered. To everyone's surprise he had employed Joyce Mahoney strictly for her musical talents, as he needed someone to play the piano; especially someone that knew older musical pieces and Joyce was certainly the right choice. Without really wanting to, he had acquired a very strong ally. For not only was Joyce pleased that Van Orsdal had asked her to be part of his theater group, her whole attitude towards him completely changed for the better. No more name calling on her part.

Penelope had agreed to let him use the parlor one night a week for a very moderate fee as long as he kept his group from being rowdy as well as not letting anyone roam around the house.

Van Orsdal told Penelope that some years ago, he had written a play, more of a satire, but had never had the opportunity of producing it. He had been too busy with teaching at the time. He needed a wide selection of trainee actors for this play. What he wanted particularly was two males and one female with good singing voices. The rest of them could be mediocre or even off-key, it didn't matter. For the play was really a comedy that would certainly have an audience laughing much of the time.

Of the fourteen people, he anticipated retaining ten, plus Joyce who would be playing the musical background where needed in all three acts of the play. Once they were sorted out ready to rehearse, he would ask some of the boarders to be the critique audience. That way he would get some feedback from their reactions.

Van Orsdal had figured that if all went fairly smoothly, the participants would be ready to rehearse as a group by August. This would give him time to make arrangements to lease a local small theater. He would also prepare publicity material to get some advertising exposure before putting the play on stage in mid-January.

'What Maddened the Gods', was finally coming alive, a reality after so many years lying dormant as a manuscript wrapped in a paper bag! A play looking for 'life'.

***

Eileen came into the dining room for breakfast one morning with her usual bubbly attitude. She greeted everyone telling them about her and Edward going on a short trip Up Island to visit places of interest. She was all happy about it just wanting to share her joy with everybody.

"This looks to me like we're going to have wedding bells in this house sooner than we expected," said Sam!

Blushing a bit, Eileen said that it was really not in the offing, as yet, with a shy smile on her face. "Edward and I are just very good friends, you know. After all he is seventy-one, getting on in years but I can assure you that he is still lively, if you know what I mean, Sam."

"Oh! Yes, I know exactly what you mean," said Sam with a twinkle in his eyes!

"Do I detect a bit of jealousy from that comment?" interjected Penelope!

"Not at all," continued Sam! "I'm just happy that Eileen has found herself a very good companion. I may have my differences with Edward, when it comes to work, but I must say that he's a very good person."

At that very moment Felicity walked in with a fresh pot of coffee and said, "Am I to understand that we are going to have a wedding soon?"

"Not as yet," said Joyce "but it's in the air. I hope that you'll be asked to prepare the food, if it happens. Anyone else would certainly not be up to the standard that you've given us in the last few months."

Felicity was obviously happy at the comments made by Joyce about her 'cheffing' as she returned to the kitchen.

Richard Taylor informed everyone that his business was finally beginning to move. Recently he had received shipments of merchandise from South America, Mexico, India and China. Clients were already buying in quantities as well as ordering for the future. "Tonight," he said, "I will provide Champagne and wine at dinner time. Please don't forget that if any of you want to look at my merchandise for reasons of purchasing for yourselves, we can make arrangements that will be convenient to all of us." On that note he got up, bade everyone farewell and left.

***

With the beginning of March, Victoria comes alive. Spring is in the air. The trees, plants and all that blooms are just about ready to burst. It's a wonderful time of the year as the weather starts getting a bit warmer. For the easterners 'touristing', it's hot. Tourists start coming back, looking for relaxation. Some to go fishing for the great salmon that western Canada is known for.

The boarding house got a bit busy too, what with the influx of 'want-to-be' actors getting together every week, it just added to the life of the place.

Penelope took in short-term tourists who had been recommended to her because they were looking for a bed & breakfast style of accommodation. This created a little more work for Felicity and Nanette as well as money for the house.

Calls for bookings of three weeks or more began to arrive from across the border and from as far east as Halifax.

As she had not done any advertising, Penelope could only deduce that people had been passing the word along. This made her feel good, the reputation of the boarding house was beginning to build in a positive way.

Penelope was sitting at her desk in the library, when the ring of the telephone startled her. She was surprised to hear the voice of Hans Kriegel, the real estate man, inquiring as to how the repairs to the old mansion were coming along.

Obviously he was either not aware that Penelope had decided to proceed with a boarding house operation, or he was just ignorant about the place, or both.

"Well," Penelope said, "all repairs, painting, rewiring along with whatever else had to be done, has been done. I'm happy to say that we're doing fine."

Kriegel went on to say that he may have a client whom might be interested in the old place. Would she consider letting him show it?

Once again, as in the Brennington case, she saw her chance to get even with this man who had really wanted her to sell the property for less than the market value.

"It's very nice of you to think of me, Mr. Kriegel, but I want you to know that I don't have any interest in selling my property right now. You see, after spending a few thousand dollars to upgrade this beautiful place, I've converted it into a boarding house. At the present time I have a few permanent guests as well as several bookings for the coming months. No, I would not be interested, but I thank you for calling," and she put the phone down. Penelope was, suddenly, overcome by laughter that really made her feel good. Kriegel had not been on the level with her, his negative attitude at the time of the inheritance had bothered her. She could now close the chapter on this incident and go on with her life.

As she was thinking about this last telephone conversation, Felicity walked into the library saying, "Just the person I was looking for!"

"What's on your mind today? Anything I can do about it for you?"

"I really don't know where to begin..." stammered Felicity.

As she was speaking, Penelope exclaimed "You're not leaving me, are you, Felicity?"

"Oh no, it's not that at all, Penelope. I made a real good friend in the last few weeks. I think its time for me to take a weekend off! Would you agree to that? Nanette is quite capable now; besides I'll have the evening meals planned for her ahead of time so that she won't have to worry. I would feel better if you could supervise her just the same. That is if you agree to my request!"

"I don't see any reason why I shouldn't. After all, you have been working so hard since we opened, haven't taken any time off at all. You deserve more than a weekend Felicity. I'll be happy to supervise Nanette as well as help in any way I can. From what you've told me about the training you've given 'your marmiton,' the guests won't even notice the difference.

"Who's the lucky man? You've been very secretive, my dear Felicity. I certainly haven't noticed any changes in your demeanor, good or bad. You always seem to have been so patient in the last few months."

"His name is Paul, he's the manager of the grocery store where Sam takes me to shop. He's about four or five years older than I am, divorced and a very nice person. I hope you'll keep this to yourself, Penelope. I'm not very good at handling teasing, especially if it were to come from Joyce Mahoney, know what I mean?"

"I certainly do," said Penelope as she remembered Joyce's tone of voice when she first mentioned the arrival of Richard Taylor.

"So, this coming weekend you'll be away. I'll put on my supervising hat already knowing that everything will work out fine. Nanette's skills have certainly improved in the past few weeks, thanks to your teaching."

Felicity left the library with a smile on her face. She almost floated down the hall to the kitchen.

Penelope was really appreciative of what Felicity had done for her boarding house operation at 13 Military Street. She went back to her books to make sure confirmations on upcoming bookings were in place in order to avoid confusion when people arrived. She decided that later on in the day while taking a break, she would take a drive towards the Gorge where Richard had his warehouse. Penelope had heard so much about it now that it was completed she wanted to see it just out of curiosity!

She took the time to complete her 'date book' once again just making sure that all was in order. She made a few telephone calls including one to Richard who told her to come by around one o'clock so they could go to lunch together.

She was feeling good about seeing Richard but still didn't want to make herself too available. More than fifteen years of comfort, love and companionship with one person was not going to disappear overnight. It would take time for her to have full confidence in her feelings towards this potential new lover. In the interim she decided to enjoy the good time this latest relationship was bringing her.

On her way to the Gorge she stopped to pick-up some cheese, a baguette along with a bottle of St-Emilion (1951). That, she thought would be a better lunch than going to a "greasy spoon" place. When she arrived at the warehouse site, she saw two cars leaving the parking lot area. As they passed her she noticed there were two men in each car. What especially caught her attention was that they looked foreign.

Knowing that Richard was in the import business she didn't dwell on this. She parked her car and walked into the warehouse where Richard was standing with a clipboard in his hands doing an inventory of some kind.

He walked towards her, gave her a hug at the same time telling her how happy he was to see her. "What was she bringing in a shopping bag?" he asked.

"Oh!" she said, "that's our lunch for today, if you don't mind! A nice bottle of red wine, two pieces of cheese, one Brie one Camembert. What do you think of that, my dear sir?"

"Let's go into my office where we can sit comfortably and enjoy this surprise. But first, let me give you a quick tour of my place. On your right is the new shipment I just received this morning from India. It's still packed in crates but trust me there are some fantastic pieces of furniture, small lamps, floor lamps in addition to different small art items that one can display in their home. Over there, as you can see, is a multitude of bamboo furniture that arrived a few days ago from Singapore. All over this floor I have items from South America, Chile and in the far corner, merchandise from Mexico."

"Wow" Penelope said, "you sure have been busy! As I arrived I saw two cars leave, were those clients or suppliers?"

"You're right on the first try, they are clients who will be purchasing from me. But, they're not from Victoria. Two are from Toronto, the other two from the States."

"I didn't mean to pry, it's really none of my business."

Richard went on, "I'm getting some catalogue items ready as you can see by the layout in this far corner. There's a photographer coming tomorrow to begin taking pictures. I hired a display lady who had worked for The Hudson Bay. She's coming in to set up and do some arranging for the photo session. Once this is all done, I should have a colorful catalogue available for my clients to purchase from. Every piece has to be numbered and defined as to size, height, etc. It's a lot of work but without it I would be restricting myself to the local market. This way, I can sell all over North America."

"That is quite an operation, Richard. I didn't realize how extensive your business is," Penelope exclaimed!

"Let's have some wine and cheese to celebrate, it's a great opportunity to do that, just the two of us," she said.

Penelope thought to herself that Richard must have spent a lot of money making his working surroundings very comfortable. When you spend twelve to sixteen hours a day at work, you have to make sure that it's commodious, she thought.

"Let's sit by the coffee table," Richard said, as he reached to put on a tablecloth he had taken from a corner cabinet where he also stored a handful of dishes, silverware and glasses.

"As you can see, Penelope, I'm prepared for my clients when they come to spend time purchasing from me."

Later, on her way home, she could not help but think how considerate this man was. Again it brought back memories of Jason McKee together with tears to her eyes. *Well*, she thought, *is it possible that I have found a 'duplicate'? Only time will tell.*

Penelope didn't have the smallest inkling as to the true nature of Richard's business. When she left the parking lot, she saw another car coming in, most likely to take a look at some merchandise. *How busy he is*, she thought. *I'm sure happy for him. It's never a sure thing when you start a new venture,* she thought while taking the road for the drive home.

That night at dinner there was champagne and wine, along with smiles from everyone. Richard insisted that Felicity take a bottle of red wine with her to the kitchen. "After all," he said, "you're part of our big family."

Reginald Van Orsdal inquired from everyone if having his students do the rehearsing in the parlor was inconvenient to them. No one seemed to mind. This old house had thick walls, and sound did not penetrate much.

After everyone had left the dining room, Penelope was alone with Richard who informed her about this coming week-end where he had some urgent business to attend to in Nanaimo but would she be free the following week-end for a trip to Seattle with him? He thought they might leave early on Friday afternoon and come back late Sunday night.

"I'm glad it's not this week-end," she said. "I gave two days off to Felicity, so I'll have to spend some time with Nanette, just to make sure everything is done right for everyone, you know. Unless something out of the ordinary occurs, I'll be very happy to go with you next week. Did you know that I have never been in Seattle? I understand that it's a well-cultured city. Yes Richard, I look forward to next weekend."

They bid each other good night. Just as Richard was going to leave, Felicity walked in saying, "Excuse me for disturbing your conversation, I just wanted to thank you for that nice bottle of French wine. Since Nanette doesn't drink I'll share it with my friend Paul this weekend."

Penelope heard the telephone ring in the library and excused herself. To her surprise, it was a call for her brother Sam from a lady with a very pleasant voice. She asked the caller if she would want to hold while she went to get Sam in the guesthouse or did she want to leave her name and number for him to call back.

The woman replied that she would stay on the line, as she needed to talk to him tonight.

Penelope put the telephone down walking towards the guesthouse to get Sam.

When he picked up the telephone, Penelope heard him say, "This is Sam, Oh hello, Jennifer, what a pleasant surprise."

She walked away to give her brother his privacy but could hardly wait to ask him who the caller was.

Once he was off the telephone, Penelope turned the television volume down as she looked at her brother and said: "Who's the new lady, Sam? "She sounded really nice as well as anxious to talk with you."

"Oh! Well," said Sam shyly, "she's a lady that I met at the store when shopping. We have talked a few times and now she wants to invite me to a B-B-Q at her house this weekend. I told her that I would be happy to come over. Her name is Jennifer Lyle, a very nice person, approximately my age, I would think. I'll invite her over next week so you can meet her in person. By the way, would you mind if I use 'Agnes' this weekend?

Jennifer lives in Central Saanich, a few miles from here, too far to walk."

Penelope told Sam that he certainly could use the car anytime he needed to. She added that she looked forward to meeting his new friend.

After Sam left the library she started to think about her personal situation, how suddenly she was becoming involved with a companion.

How about Felicity, she thought, *it seems that we're all being matched up somehow. So far this house has been good to many of us but I must not forget my business obligations, they are my first priority.*

She turned off the television as well as the lights, walked upstairs to her own bedroom with thoughts on her mind about her brother, Felicity and Richard Taylor. There was something about this man that she could not figure out. For instance, who he really was? And why open an import/export business in Victoria? The population pool was certainly not his main reason for being here. So many questions she wished she knew the answers to.

Those answers would eventually come to her but not in a pleasant way!

CHAPTER THIRTEEN…

The time she had been looking for finally arrived. Penelope was packing her week-ender bag for the trip to Seattle with Richard.

At breakfast she again asked Felicity to keep an eye on things. Her brother Sam would also be available if needed. The boarding house was being left in good hands. She told Felicity she would be back on the last ferry Sunday night. "Get Sam to give you the telephone number where he's going to be spending his time this week-end, just in case."

Just as she was getting ready to leave the dining room, Joyce and Van Orsdal walked in both smiling with a happy look on their faces. *What a difference*, Penelope thought. *A few months ago they were at each other's throats, now they're almost 'kissing cousins'. I guess the old charmer got his way by the look of things, his play is coming along really well. This house sure has an influence on people's behavior. I wouldn't have thought the day would come when these two would be holding hands! It's almost a miracle.*

"Good morning Miss Woodspring," said Van Orsdal with all the charm he could muster.

"Well," said Penelope "Everyone appears to be in a cheerful mood this morning. Any special reasons why? How is your work, or should I say 'play', coming along Mr. Van Orsdal?"

"My dear lady, I'm very fortunate to have chosen, in some remarkable way, what I think to be the right players for this little masterpiece of mine. Having Miss Mahoney handle the music side of it, plus acting as my assistant, has surely made life a bit easier for me. I must also say that the surroundings in which we're working are conducive to excellence at the same time. This house, including the parlor you had the generosity to allow us to use, is the inspiration for my group."

"Thank you, Mr. Van Orsdal, I'm happy to see that all is going well for you. I look forward to seeing your play on stage early next year," smiled Penelope.

She also thought, *What a flatterer this man is. He pours it on so heavily at times that it makes you wonder if he really means what he's saying.*

"I'll be away this week-end so if you're in need of anything, please ask Felicity, I'm sure she'll be happy to help in any way she can," she informed them.

***

Richard Taylor had taken a drive near the water in Oak Bay to have a look at small pleasure boats. He spotted a 'for sale' sign, parked the car and walked to where the boat was moored amongst many others. It caught his attention, as it appeared to be about 36 feet in length, was wooden with a natural lacquer finish. Someone standing nearby noticed he was looking at the boat and asked him if he wanted to look inside.

"I would certainly like to," Richard said. "How is it powered?"

"It has two diesel engines, designed for high seas as well as being only five years old. My father bought it when he retired, thinking that he and mother would go exploring the coast from here to Mexico. Unfortunately he had a fatal heart attack three months ago," the stranger stated.

"I'm sorry to hear that, but why would you want to sell such a beautiful boat?" asked Richard.

"I don't have sea legs. Just sitting on deck with the soft movement of the waves, I get seasick," said the man. "Besides, I'm moving back to Toronto in a few weeks. Mother has decided to come along, too. The rest of our family is all back East. It'll be better for our mother to be with every one."

The boat could sleep six, was fully equipped, just like a floating miniature cottage. The more Richard looked at it, the more he became convinced he had to have this wonderful toy, though in his mind, it was not strictly for pleasure but rather for 'business'.

"Before you tell me what you're asking for this vessel, can you tell me where I could learn or take a course in navigation? Is there someone available I could hire to teach me all about 'driving' a boat?" asked Richard.

"The Coast Guard office is the best place to inquire about the navigation aspect I would think, but I'm sure the man at the boathouse could give you more information," replied the man.

"By the way I'm Jonathan Smiley. Since you'll want to know, we're asking $22,500.00 in order to sell it fast."

"I'm Richard Taylor," said Richard as he handed Jonathan his business card.

"Can someone take me for a short ride, say for half an hour, so that I can get a feel for this boat. I'm very much interested. If I'm satisfied, you'll be looking at a cash sale."

"I'll certainly find someone to take you out with the boat but I can't do that until tomorrow. May I call you at this number, Mr. Taylor, let's say around nine-thirty tomorrow morning, if it's convenient for you?" said Jonathan.

"That'll be fine with me Mr. Smiley, I look forward to your call. In the meantime I'll make some inquiries with the man at the boathouse."

Richard was already planning to dock the boat at his own facility. He would have an overhead hanger built in order to have access to the boat without having to stand outside in inclement weather. Yes, his place was perfect with the new dock, he was sure he would find his way around the Gorge Waterway without any hassle. On that thought he went back to his car making sure to note Smiley's telephone number on the 'for sale' sign. Richard would give Smiley a call later in the evening to inquire if he had found someone who would teach him navigational skills.

After his weekend in Seattle with Penelope, he now had found another way to use her in his "cover-up" activities.

***

The next morning his office telephone rang and Jonathan Smiley told him that he had located a Tom McMillan, an old sea captain friend of his father who was willing to take him out for an hour or so at his convenience. "When would you like to do this?" Smiley asked.

"If you can give me his name again and telephone number I'll make arrangements with him right now. I'll get back to you once we're back at your mooring place," said Richard. This was right up Richard's alley; somehow his luck was almost too good to be true!

He phoned Tom McMillan just before noon, and made the arrangements to meet him at the boathouse in Oak Bay at about two o'clock that day.

***

McMillan looked like an old sea-going man in his middle to late sixties. He told Richard that as a Captain on a cargo ship he had traveled the world. Yes, he was familiar with getting into the Gorge Waterway and would be glad to show him.

Richard was very impressed with the way McMillan operated the small vessel. As they neared Richard's place, he asked him to dock right in front of his warehouse on which there was a huge sign, "TAYLOR IMPORT/EXPORT."

"Well," said the captain, "this is a very nice docking facility that you have here. It looks brand new, did you just have it built?"

"I certainly did," said Richard. "But it is intended for larger boats from all over the world with merchandise for my business. It's quite handy I must say. This beautiful boat will be a wonderful addition to use in my leisure time which I intend to have a lot of as my business becomes better established!"

They were back at the Oak Bay boathouse within the hour. Richard immediately went to telephone Jonathan Smiley.

The deal was completed that afternoon and Richard hired old McMillan to get the boat to the warehouse facilities as well as giving him a few lessons on the operation of this magnificent, expensive toy. He then made arrangements with the Coast Guard for a course in navigation training.

***

Penelope was sitting at her desk in the library just reminiscing about her trip to Seattle a couple of weeks before and how it had been so pleasant to be with someone whose company you enjoyed.

She remembered the theater and how wonderful it had been listening to the Philadelphia Symphony Orchestra playing the best of Mozart. The whole weekend had been like a dream. When they were alone at bedtime, how attentive Richard had been. What a good lover he was. She couldn't help but make a mental comparison with Jason, whom she could not really forget. Still, there was something she could not put her finger on, something gnawing at the back of her mind telling her to be careful with this relationship.

What the careful meant, she wasn't sure but it was bothering her. If only she could put her finger on it. "Oh! Well," she said to herself, "I'll ask some questions and maybe I'll get some answers. I wonder about his parents, relatives, etc. He never talks about that part of his background." The ringing of the telephone put an end to her daydreaming.

"I was just thinking about you. Richard, how nice of you to call", she said. "Certainly I would like to come over to your business place to have lunch. Would you like me to bring some wine and cheese? OK, as you wish, I'll just bring little old me. Is one o'clock fine with you?"

"It certainly is," said Richard again reminding her not to bring anything as he had sufficient supplies for lunch.

I wonder what he has in mind, thought Penelope! *Good surprises are always uplifting.* She left it at that.

Penelope walked into the kitchen and saw that Felicity and Nanette were just working up a storm. "What's going on?" she said, "are we preparing something special?"

"Not at all," said Felicity! "We are just keeping up with our steady flow of new tourists. Do you realize that for the last four weeks we've had six extra people a week? That's good for the boarding house. I hope it keeps going in that direction, then we won't get rusty in here."

"As if you would," said Penelope. "I will not be here for lunch today. Just thought of asking if there was anything I could bring home on my way back?"

"Thank you for asking but I've already been to the market with Sam an hour ago," said Felicity.

Penelope went to her room, got herself ready and departed for her trip to the Gorge Waterway to a pleasant lunchtime with a man who just made her feel good all over.

On her way there she thought again of asking him about his family. When she got to the warehouse and parked the car she noticed a new addition to the docking facility she had not seen before. It was shaped like a hangar, rather like a carport, but thought nothing of it.

As she walked into the warehouse Richard was waiting for her with a smile on his face. She wondered what he was up to.

He greeted her with a hug as well as a kiss, telling her there was no reason for them to hang around. He took hold of her arm and walked outside towards the end of the dock where a boat was tied under this hangar type roof.

"Let me show you my new acquisition," he said with a big grin.

She couldn't believe her eyes when she saw the shiny, pretty boat. "When did you get this?" she asked in an awe-struck tone. "It's just so beautiful."

"Climb aboard and meet the Captain; we're going to have lunch on the water today, my dear Penelope," said Richard smiling.

After introducing her to Captain McMillan, he showed her where to sit, the engine revved loudly. Richard's boat was on its way out of the waterway to the open sea.

"I certainly hope you don't get sea-sick. I wanted this to be a surprise so I couldn't tell you anything about it before- hand," said Richard.

"What a surprise," Penelope said. "It's just wonderful. Besides, I love boating."

"We're just going to drive around the point, then proceed into the inner harbor so that you can have a look at how Victoria appears to someone arriving from a voyage out at sea."

Penelope could not believe her eyes. The sun was shining brightly and here she was with a lover who gave her more attention than she could ever hope to receive. Furthermore, she thought, money appeared to be no object.

They had a wonderful private lunch inside the cabin while Captain McMillan kept the boat steady. Richard told her he needed to enjoy some relaxation. The Captain was only hired temporarily to teach him how to safely maneuver the boat until he could take a month's technical training with the Coast Guard. "With this boat," he said "we can go anywhere along the coast of Vancouver Island or anywhere else we would want to go. It's a very safe boat. With its two engines in addi-

tion to an extra large fuel reserve tank we can navigate far without having to fill up so often. You
know, Penelope, you – along with this Island –
seem to bring me good luck. I purchased this boat
on the spur of the moment from an individual who
needed to sell it fast before moving back to Toronto. It belonged to his father who passed away a
few months ago. The man told me he was not the
sailing type! Besides, I had the feeling he needed
the cash. Since he was not asking too high a price,
I made him an immediate offer, which he accepted. Even the Captain told me that she's worth
more than double that on the open market."

"My dear Richard, this is almost like a
dream. I have the feeling that if I pinch myself I'm
going to wake-up."

"Be assured that it's reality Penelope! I also have a little something for you that I could not
have given you at the boarding house. I wanted a
special occasion. I think this is it," as he handed
her a small gift-wrapped package.

"Oh! Richard, you didn't have to do that,"
she said as she started to open the package.
"Wow!" Penelope exclaimed as she looked in the
box to find a double string of pearls necklace.

"How beautiful!" she exclaimed.

"Let me place them around your neck,
that's where they belong, my beautiful lady," said
Richard smiling.

The rest of the outing was just fantastic.
They returned to the dock at Taylor's Im-
port/Export after just under two hours of boating
pleasure.

On her way home Penelope was still mar-veling about the gift she had just received. She thought that Richard must have spent a few hun-dred dollars to buy such a lovely pearl necklace. Penelope had not been able to pursue her idea of inquiring about his family. She would choose an-other time more appropriate for that kind of pri-vate conversation.

As she walked into the library of the boarding house, she was greeted by Felicity who handed her three telephone messages while asking her how her lunch trip had gone.

"It could not have been better, Felicity I'll tell you more about it later on. My mind is still 'buzzing' but now I have to put my business hat on. Life is full of surprises! Isn't it?"

One of the messages was from Hanna Mueller who was calling from San Francisco. She decided to return that call first.

Miss Mueller wanted to inform her that her friend Liz Traynor was coming to Victoria with her. "Would it be possible to have rooms on the same floor?"

Penelope assured her that her request would be taken care of as wished. She told her she looked forward to seeing her again in a couple of weeks.

The next two calls had to do with suppliers with whom her brother Sam had placed orders for needed materials to repair part of the roof.

She sat at her desk and started to daydream again about her "affair" with Richard Taylor, but for some unknown reason, she kept reminding herself to go at it carefully.

***

After breakfast one morning when everyone had left to go about his or her business, Eileen found that she was alone with Penelope, and said, "May I talk to you for a moment?"

"You certainly may, what's on your mind?"

"Edward and I have finally decided on a wedding date."

"That's fabulous," said Penelope. "When is it?"

"We thought the first of August would be a good time since my daughter, grandchildren as well as my son with his wife could all make it at that time. Edward does not have any relatives left so he was happy that I should decide it all."

Just then, Felicity walked in. Penelope blurted out what Eileen had just finished telling her.

In her usual shy manner Eileen asked Felicity if she would stand as her maid of honor.

"Who's going to prepare the food for the reception if I agree to do that?" asked Felicity.

"Edward and I want it to be as simple as can be. We're not spring chickens anymore, as you know. The companionship is the most important for us. I thought of saving you a whole lot of work by asking you to choose the best caterer in town, just have it delivered right here. We want this to be an early afternoon affair so as not to disturb the daily routine of this house."

Penelope interrupted by saying they were not interfering with anything at the boarding house. "We're very happy to provide a place for your wedding reception. I think it will be a great event for this boarding house. Don't you agree, Felicity?"

"I certainly do, moreover if you tell me that you would like a caterer to handle the food, it's fine with me. It'll give me more time to socialize. I'm sure my friend Paul will be happy," answered Felicity.

"So," said Penelope, "we are all in agreement as to the reception including where we're having it. How many people do you intend to invite Eileen?"

"I'll have a full list ready in a few days. If there is anyone else you would want to add to the list, just go ahead. I need to talk to your brother Sam to see if he'll agree to be Edward's best man. Is he around the house right now?"

"I think he's gone to do a few errands, but he'll be back soon, I imagine. I'll let him know that you want to talk with him."

Eileen reached in her purse handing Felicity five hundred dollars in cash. "This is for the catering order, if you need more, just let me know. By the way, Edward and I are looking at purchasing a house in Oak Bay in the next week or so, I'll let you know in time. I don't want to move away from here until after the wedding, that is, if you agree to that, Penelope."

At dinner that evening, everyone was told about the up-coming wedding of Eileen and Edward. Everyone gave congratulations. Reginald Van Orsdal was especially happy for this lady whom he admired so much for her forthright manner. "She is a breath of fresh air that this house will certainly miss. But," he added, "I wish you all the happiness in the world."

Two bottles of Champagne were set on the table as a toast was in order. Richard did the honors and they all settled down for a lively dinner.

Sam was delighted that he had been asked to be the groom's best man. He was looking forward to the wedding day.

***

The following week was a busy one for the management of the boarding house. Summer was here, new guests were arriving making it a full house. Penelope had to give a hand with the cleaning of rooms in order to keep the operation running as smoothly as possible.

On July 1, Hanna Mueller along with her friend Liz Traynor arrived. They were greeted by Sam who took the luggage up to the third floor rooms. Hanna was quite pleased to see she was being given the same room she had so enjoyed a few short months ago. She asked Sam to wait around for a moment; she wanted to give him a copy of the photograph he had taken of her on the Gorge Waterway.

Needless to say he was very pleased, telling her that he would have it framed to keep it on his dresser.

When Richard Taylor came home that night to find that Miss Mueller was back in Victoria so soon, he got a bit suspicious. He decided to make a telephone call to his associate Gabby Vito in Montreal. Maybe they could do a more substantial check on this person. He could not really afford to have anything go wrong in his operation. Personally he was as clean as a whistle, no police record of any kind, not even an arrest for speeding. Yes, the return of this lady puzzled him. On the other hand, he was not going to lose any sleep over it or act differently. It may just be pure chance that she decided to come back here with a friend. If not, he would soon find out and may have to use the services of Gino Saturno as had been suggested to him.

He quickly thought of a plan that would certainly help him to keep an eye on her as well as her friend. "Why not," he said to himself. "I'll take a few ladies out on my boat for an afternoon of sightseeing, in that way it will keep everything in perspective. No one will suspect my true reasons for doing so. Now I must go into town to find a pay phone to call Gabby."

***

Richard was a little late returning to the dining room for dinner but showed no sign of nervousness. He greeted Miss Mueller with a pleasant smile, adding he was a bit surprised at

seeing her back in Victoria so soon. He was introduced to her friend Liz Traynor. The regular dinner chatter kept everyone occupied.

Hanna told him that she had liked Victoria
so much she wanted her friend to enjoy it, too.
They would do the regular tourists attractions as
well as explore the Island a bit more.

Richard took the opportunity to tell the
regular boarders he had received a boatload of
new furnishings from India about a week ago.
Most of it was now unpacked on the warehouse
floor if anyone was interested in purchasing something as he had promised he would let them do.

Joyce Mahoney asked if it would be convenient for her to drop by tomorrow, that is, if
Sam was able to drive her there?

"Not a problem," said Sam "I'll be happy
to take anyone who wants to go to Mr. Taylor's
place of business. Just let me know when you're
ready to do so."

Van Orsdal said that he would like to take
a look, too. Not sure if he would purchase anything, but satisfy his curiosity.

***

The following morning as Richard was
getting ready to go for breakfast, his telephone
suddenly rang, and he picked it up answering,
"Taylor here!" A voice he recognized told him
that his information turned out to be negative.
Everything was on the up and up, not to worry but
was very glad that he was careful. Richard said

thank you without mentioning a name just in case his telephone was being watched.

Everyone was in a cheerful mood at the breakfast table. Richard surprised them all by offering the ladies an outing in his new boat this Sunday if they would like to go.

Hanna was the first to answer positively. She thought it was very gentlemanly of him to make such an offer hoping it would not inconvenience him too much.

"Not at all," said Richard. "I purchased this thirty-six footer a few weeks ago. I may just as well use it while the weather is so pleasant. By the way, no need to be concerned about navigation, I've hired a retired sea captain who will guide us along until I have the opportunity to complete the thirty-day instructional navigational course from the Coast Guard."

Hanna found it very interesting that Malouf (Richard) had purchased a boat. *How convenient,* she thought! *He can cruise the coast without hindrance from anyone and most likely arrange meetings or exchanges on the water. Well,* she thought again, *after the Sunday boat excursion I'll certainly inform my superiors of these new developments.*

Since this was only Thursday, there was time enough to discuss the whole thing with her partner, Liz Traynor. They must act the tourist part for the next couple of days. They certainly did not want to attract attention as to their real purpose for being there. *What an opportunity. Here we are going to be on this boat, able to look at it*

carefully without having to worry about being de-
tected! It could not have happened in a better way.
A bit of luck is always welcome in these investiga-
tions. "Besides," she said to herself, "we'll have
the chance to look at the inside of his warehouse.
That, in itself, should be very revealing." As her
superiors had not received any additional information from their sources, she and Liz had been
asked to snoop around to see what they could find.
They had been told about the disappearance of
Laurent Lemay some weeks ago plus that it would
take some months before another mole could be
planted in the Vitriolli crime family. It was up to
Hanna and Liz to gather as much information as
they could.

***

The last two days of the week went by sat-
isfactorily. The two Californian ladies visited
Butchart Gardens in addition to spending all of
Saturday in downtown Victoria. They even had
tea at the Empress Hotel as well as visiting the
Legislative buildings.

When everyone was at breakfast on Sunday morning, Richard wanted to know who was
coming along for the short cruise. "Does everyone
know where my warehouse is?"

Sam stated that he would be the lead car
and take them there for ten o'clock as scheduled.

When they all arrived at the docking facility, Richard was there with Captain McMillan to
greet everyone before climbing aboard the beautiful 36-foot cruiser. He introduced the ladies.

"Here's Penelope whom you already know, this is Mrs. Eileen Flowers soon to be Mrs. Edward Stone. This lady is Felicity Potts. our wonderful chef; Miss Joyce Mahoney, our entertainment committee and I must add, a very good piano player. Our two visitors from the United States; Miss Hanna Mueller and Miss Elizabeth Traynor. Ladies this is Captain Tom McMillan who has forty years of sea-going experience. We're in safe hands as you can see. Does anyone here suffer from seasickness? Don't be afraid to say so because I have a remedy in the cabin that will take care of it for you. There's sufficient room for everyone to sit on the deck but you're free to roam around. First, let me show you where the life jackets are in case of an emergency. Here is where the food and drinks are stored in the cabin section.

"We're going to be gone from shore for approximately three hours. Is everyone OK with that?" No one objected as the Captain started the engine for the great adventure to begin.

As they went out of the Gorge Waterway they could see many sailboats all over the Strait of Juan de Fuca. With the slight wind, it was an ideal day for sailing. In the powerboat, it was such a smooth ride the cruiser seemed to be floating above the water.

The Captain anchored in the channel between James Island and Sidney Island. This was an excellent spot to have lunch. Richard had a fishing pole aboard; he tried a little fishing from the side of the boat. Surprisingly after four tries, he brought in two beautiful salmon, which he turned over to Felicity for the next dinner at the Boarding House.

The return journey was fast without any incidents. They docked at two-thirty, a bit later than originally intended. Richard then showed everyone the warehouse and its contents.

Hanna Mueller jumped on the opportunity to take a few pictures for future reference. *What a break,* she thought. *The investigating team will appreciate a look at the premises without compromising anyone.*

What most of these people on this boat ride did not realize were the conniving abilities of one Richard Taylor!

CHAPTER FOURTEEN…

After the Sunday boat ride, Hanna and her friend Liz were going over the events of the past week including the famous Sunday trip as well as the visit to the warehouse. They each had bought a couple of different items from Richard. They were still trying to figure out how he imported the drugs in the country. Where did he store them? What quantities did he receive? For both of them, these were the important questions. They realized he must have a plan for quickly passing the drugs to a major distributor. The next phase was the moving of the drugs from his point of reception. Did he have a group of trusted runners?

"No," Hanna said, "I don't think he has had time to set that up yet. During the next week, we should keep an eye on him, see where he goes including with whom he meets."

"How do we find out if he has received any shipments of drugs from South America?" asked Liz. "Do we have any international inform-ers who could help us in some way?"

"We're not set up for that yet," said Hanna. "The boss only wants us to snoop around for now. Lets gain Mr. Taylor's confidence. If we're too inquisitive he may get suspicious of us possibly putting an end to our cover. We can't afford to lose this one, we have to exercise patience, a lot of patience since this man is so crafty," concluded Hanna Mueller.

"Our Canadian counterparts should be able to dig something up in Montreal. The Vito family is related to the infamous Leonardo Arminto of New York! We have to remember this, including placing a trail in that direction. We might get lucky in our search on the US side of things."

For the rest of the week the two ladies played it safe by doing what normal tourists would do. This was to avoid arousing Taylor's suspicions.

At dinner on Friday night they told everyone this was their last evening together as tomorrow was going-home day. Both Hanna and Liz expressed their special thanks to Richard for his kindness towards them. Hanna repeated how they had enjoyed last Sunday's boat trip. She added that Victoria was really a wonderful place to spend a relaxing time. They were both returning home with great memories.

Hanna thought, what a hypocrite this Taylor (Malouf) is. How convincing he is, the perfect conman. I wish I had a way to warn Penelope Woodspring about him but I can't at this time. This lady has no idea how dangerous the man is. No one had any idea how these drug dealers would eliminate anyone that stood in their way. It had already happened back East with the disappearance of the RCMP's top informer. I know this lady is definitely not involved in his drug business.

Hanna's name being called brought her out of her rêverie.

"Well," said Penelope, "you were sure far away, Miss Mueller! Thinking about what tomorrow will bring? As my old mother used to say, 'Let tomorrow come when it does, just deal with it'. She always added to that; 'you cannot worry about things that may not happen'. It has taken me until very recently in my life to understand that. There are moments when I wish I could predict the future," she said.

How can this lady be so intuitive and not see through this man? Those were Hanna's thoughts at that moment.

"So sorry," Hanna said. "I was just thinking about my agenda. I'm sure glad I had these last two weeks to relax a bit, it makes it easier to keep going."

"I would be happy to take you two ladies to the airport," said Sam.

"Thank you very much Sam," Hanna smiled. "There's no need for it as we have to return the rented car prior to our departure."

"We wish you a safe trip home," said Penelope. "Please return anytime you want to. You're always welcome in our house."

***

The wedding of Eileen and Edward was less than a week away. The preparations were well underway. There would be about twenty people in all. The food had been ordered at Jean-François' catering service, which was known in Victoria as the best French cuisine around. There would be Champagne, plenty of wine for the guests. Jean-François had insisted, for no extra cost, to be the Maître D' in person.

Penelope had reserved three rooms on the third floor for Eileen's relatives. She would not accept a penny for it. "This," she said, "is part of my present to you. After all, you've been part of our family for some time now."

***

The wedding reception went smoothly. It was a beautiful sunny day. The guests were able to move around from the house to the front lawn. Penelope had purchased several pieces of lawn furniture from an auction sale along with some beautiful rattan pieces at wholesale prices from Richard. It was, indeed, a scene from the past with the children playing in addition to running in and out of the house. It took Penelope's thoughts back to her youth on her parent's farm just a few miles out of Calgary.

Felicity was delighted that the catering service was well organized. The fact that she didn't have to do it herself made it even more enjoyable.

Labor Day was just around the corner and the weather was very warm in Victoria. As a matter of fact it was still summery. The weather forecast to be so for some time yet.

Eileen had moved out of the boarding house and was now living in Oak Bay. Mr. and Mrs. Stone appeared to be the happiest couple in the world. Their honeymoon had been spent up Island at a resort in a very peaceful setting.

Things were running smoothly at 13 Military Street, people were settled, guests were coming and going. It was, indeed, a very busy time; a time that kept Penelope occupied so sufficiently she didn't have to think about her relationship with Richard Taylor. That, for the moment, suited her just fine.

Reginald Van Orsdal was preparing an evening rehearsal performance of his play. He made it known at mealtime that they were all invited, as he needed some feed- back in order to make necessary adjustments to the play!

The busy time was really the quiet before the storm that no one knew was coming to the boarding house.

***

In Ottawa, Chief Inspector Hector Lesage had received some information from Gerald Smudgely, FBI bureau Chief in Los Angeles, about an intended meeting to update everyone on the developments of the last few weeks. Lesage was looking forward to such a meeting. It seemed the trail had gone cold on the Canadian side since the disappearance of Laurent Lemay. (Lying in his concrete tomb at the bottom of the St-Lawrence River.)

Even around-the-clock surveillance on Gabby Vito, including some of his associates, had brought nothing unusual. They were operating nightclubs in the greater Montreal area where every move they made appeared to be within the law. That in itself was not normal for the Vito family. They were usually breaking the law whenever surveillance was placed on them. The Inspector figured that 'something big' must be coming up or going to happen in the near future, he didn't want to miss any part of it.

Patience was the most important aspect of this investigation. A wrong move too soon would unquestionably be costly for the law enforcement agency. Months after months of preparation, not to mention the cost, would go down the drain if their timing was wrong. For that reason they let a lot of petty stuff slip by without interference in order to encourage the perpetrator's confidence.

Margot Helmsway had not gathered much more additional information than they already had. Inspector Lesage could not take the chance of sending her again to Victoria taking the risk to have her cover blown. No, that was too risky! The up-coming meeting in Los Angeles might reveal more interesting information from the FBI. Some new information would allow him to re-examine his strategy if necessary, thus making some progress.

Acting on that premise, he got his secretary to book his flight to Los Angeles and make the necessary reservations for two days hence. At the same time, he picked up the telephone to call Bureau Chief Smudgely to let him know that he was coming down for the meeting.

The afternoon before his departure, one of his undercover officers called him to report that he had some important information from the police surveillance on the Vito family group. The Inspector told the officer to meet him at the office after seven that night.

Lesage could not believe his luck when he met with the young officer. A close member of the Vito family was apparently dissatisfied with the organization. Luciano Miranzino, known by his nickname of 'Lucky,' was not happy about the secretive meetings held by the 'family' without his participation. One evening after having had a few drinks he talked openly to the young under-cover officer about his disenchantment including the way that Gabby was not keeping him informed on the drug operation out of South America. Some shipments were apparently coming into North America through the West Coast somehow.

Officer Delaney told the Inspector that he didn't question Lucky on this subject, but rather lent a listening ear to his gripes. "That way," he said, "he was not suspicious of me and more open to spill his guts. Perhaps his frustration as well as his greed can be a big help to us if we take the time to be patient," he added, "even though it would be useful to find everything out at once if I push it."

Chief Inspector Lesage asked the officer if he saw any possibility about this person becoming a solid informer?

"I think so Sir, but it will take some very careful handling", Delaney replied. "We don't want to lose another key informer like we lost Lemay. I just wanted to report that there is a possibility of a breakthrough. It will take time if you allow me to work on it. If you agree, could you please ask all other team members not to interfere at this time? This will be a very sensitive situation that could jeopardize the whole operation if things were to go wrong."

"You certainly have some very interesting as well as valuable information, Delaney," commented the happy-faced Inspector. "Have you talked this over with anyone else on the team yet?"

"No Sir, you're the first and only person," replied the officer.

"Well done, young man," said Lesage. "I sure appreciate your good work. I want you to strengthen your relationship with this 'Lucky' guy without arousing his suspicious nature. When I return from my trip to Los Angeles it might be appropriate, perhaps to meet with you again. This time include some other members of the team in our plans. Together I'm sure we'll find a solution to our present predicament. Who knows, this may be the break we have been looking for." With those words, they shook hands and left the office going in separate directions.

*** voila

Before going to sleep that night, Hector Lesage was mentally going through, step by step, the possible implications the conversation with Officer Delaney might have as a result of his findings. He thought that finally here was an opportunity for them to move forward in their search.

His American associates would be pleased with this possible break-through! Getting someone from inside the Vito family to open up had so far been an impossible task, but now, with luck on their side for once, things might change.

***

Penelope was sitting alone finishing a second cup of coffee when Richard walked into the dining room. "Good morning, Richard," she said smiling. "I want to thank you for all the kindness that you showed everyone lately. I mean, the boat ride was just outstanding, not to mention the visit to your warehouse, which was really enjoyed by all. I just feel at a loss to express my gratitude."

Then coyly she added, "Can I get you some breakfast?"

"Yes you can," he replied, "you've expressed your gratitude towards me already perhaps in more ways than you realize. I'm wondering if you have some free time this weekend? I'm planning a boat trip to Tofino by myself; no captain this time. I would love to have you on as my co-captain. Does that sound like a good outing for you or did you have other things in mind?"

"That is the best invitation I've had today," she blurted out. "How can I refuse what would appear to be an extremely pleasant get-away?" With these words she went to the kitchen to ask Nanette if she would mind serving Mr. Taylor his breakfast. She returned to the dining room to inquire from Richard when he wanted to leave, morning or afternoon on Friday?

"Friday morning would be perfect," said Richard, "if it's OK with you. The marine weather office informed me that we should have calm seas in both directions. I thought of returning Sunday afternoon, is that fine with you?"

Penelope was happy to accept the invitation. This time she would find a way to question him about his family, where he was born, went to school, etc., so she thought!

After Richard left for work, she went to the library to update her bookings, check all reservations as well as make sure that nothing had been forgotten. Life was going well, indeed.

Sam joined his sister in the library, took a seat and just sat there not saying a word or making a sound. She was so absorbed in her books and thinking about her up-coming trip with Richard that she did not hear Sam walk in. As she turned around she was startled to see Sam sitting there so quietly. "What's the matter, little brother?" She inquired. "Are you not feeling well?"

"Oh! No I'm very well," he replied. "It's just that Jennifer has asked me to spend the weekend up Island with her. I really don't know what to do. You know I'm a bit shy and awkward when it comes to women. Being together all weekend means that we will have to be in the same bedroom, share the same bed and all that. It's been a long time since I was intimate with a woman. Not since my own wife ran away eight years ago. You're the only one that knows that, Penelope. What do you think I should do?"

Penelope really felt sorry for her brother. She understood the reasoning behind it all. After his wife had left he had filed for divorce, Sam had been very broken up. It was shortly following that incident while working on a construction site when this terrible accident happened to him. It left Sam unable to continue working full time as a carpenter. He had not been the same person since. She thought quickly and said to him, "Why don't you invite Jennifer to dinner tonight. That'll give me a chance to meet her then I'll be in a better position to give you advice, if you still want me to."

"Since you put it that way, I think I'll do just that," Sam replied. He walked over to the desk, picked up the telephone dialing Jennifer's number.

Penelope was pleased to see that her brother reacted in a positive way. She knew him so well she could read him like an open book. He just needed a little nudge to get out of his shell. The little sister saw no reason for not being the 'nudgor.'

***

That evening at dinner, introductions were made all around; everyone doing their best to make Jennifer feel part of the family.

Sam was proud to introduce his lady friend to the regulars of the boarding house. Jennifer was a petite brunette with unusual piercing blue eyes in addition to a ready smile. She was a bit talkative, but that could have been a nervous reaction to all 'these people' looking her over.

After dinner when the guests had left, Penelope invited Jennifer and Sam to the library for a second cup of coffee to go with a snifter of "Grande Fine Champagne Napoleon," the best cognac the world over.

Sam did the honors for the two ladies but passed for himself. He added that liquor did not agree with him. It did upset his stomach, besides he really didn't like anything stronger than wine.

Penelope got along very well with Jennifer. Their conversation flowed for more than an hour. Sam was delighted that his sister appeared to like his new lady friend. It was very important to him that his sister gave the approval about the new companion since he had no other family. He didn't want her disapproval; he wanted his sister to like the lady of his choice.

Later that evening when Sam returned home he noticed that a light was still on in the library. He walked in to find his sister seated comfortably reading a book.

"Well" he said, "what did you think of Jennifer?"

"I must be honest with you Sam, she's a nice lady and pretty as well," Penelope answered. "You're a lucky man whether you know it or not. If you still want my opinion about your weekend trip, I'll gladly give it to you."

"That's exactly why I came to talk to you in the first place, so please don't hesitate to tell me what I should do."

Poor Sam, she thought, *so unsure of himself.* "Dear brother, if I was in your shoes I would not think twice about spending the weekend with this lovely lady! Does that answer you?"

Sam went to bed that night feeling like a new man.

***

Friday morning was already here. Penelope was ready for the boat trip. She was looking forward to being alone with Richard for a change. There were so many questions left unanswered, which were bothersome to her. She felt that being alone with him would bring the opportunity she had been looking for.

Everyone at the boarding house knew that Penelope spent time with Richard Taylor but no one dared to comment. Felicity had been asked again to take care of the business, while she was away. In an emergency Felicity would call Edward who had been kind enough to leave his new telephone number with them since Sam was away at the same time.

Richard was in a charming mood, more so today because he had successfully passed the technical part of the navigation course given by the Coast Guard. He wanted to prove to himself that he could handle this boat alone under all circumstances. This trip was a test, a real test for him, looking into the future to probable forthcoming business deals.

Penelope watched him handle the preparations for departure from the dock. There was a lot to do if one wanted to carry out the safety rules taught in the course. Richard had given her a small booklet that explained the procedures to follow prior to starting a diesel engine on a boat. He also asked her to keep an eye on him to make sure he did not omit any step that should be taken.

Once they were out of the Harbor, Richard followed the coast of Vancouver Island at a short distance from the coastline. The view was just out of this world. Cutting through the calm seas was like sliding down a soft powdered ski hill.

After an hour of travel he decided to slow down, come closer to shore and anchor so that he could prepare coffee and croissants for both of them.

While he was making coffee Penelope was deep in thought trying to work out how to begin to question him without aggravating him, the last thing she wanted to happen.

After a kiss with some passionate embraces Richard asked her if she felt comfortable.

"I am indeed, Richard," she said smiling. "It's so calm and private out here on the water that I never realized how peaceful as well as pleasant it could be. Did you go boating a lot when you were a child?"

"My father had a big yacht, twice the size of this boat," he said. "He used to take me along with my mother on weekend trips. Since he had a crew of five aboard, there wasn't anything for him to actually physically do. He taught me how to play chess during those weekends. These learning vacations were frequent enough for me to become quite good at the game of chess, even besting some adults on many occasions. You told me the first time we were on this boat that you had done a lot of boating in the past, were you on cruises or pleasure boats of some kind?"

Penelope said she did both cruises on large ships as well as some pleasure boating. "What I enjoyed most was house-boat trips that you could take. Traveling up and down the locks from Kingston, Ontario to Ottawa. It's an experience one should have at least once in a lifetime. I also enjoyed sailing but one needs to have an experienced sailor or it could be disastrous."

Richard must have sensed that she wanted to question him because spontaneously as he was serving the coffee and croissants, he started to tell her the story of his youth. He obviously lied to her because he didn't want Penelope to know he was not who he said he was. He needed her to believe in his alias. Richard was a smooth talker; the story that he made up about his early life in Montreal was believable since he spoke French fluently. He told her his mother was Lebanese, that his father was Irish. Actually it was the reverse but since she did not know him under his real name he presumed that she would never find out. He knew from the beginning that she was naïve which suited him just fine. He said his father had a large import/export business, mostly fabrics he sold to the "clothing-trade" in Montreal. The father would sometime sell in Western Canada as well. To make more of an impression on her, he told Penelope his parents had been killed in a car accident twelve years ago when the driver of a transport truck had fallen asleep at the wheel driving right on top of them killing both parents instantly.

Penelope was almost in a state of shock after hearing that. Seeing the sad look on Richard's face, she decided not to question him any further.

Suddenly there were noises coming from the rear of the boat. As they both looked, they saw a group of sea lions just waiting for them to throw something overboard. That distraction just played into Richard's hand. He pulled-up the anchor, started the engine heading a little further out to sea in order to motor on towards their destination. The wind caused by the boat speeding through the water was a bit cool so Penelope got herself a wrap to keep warm.

By late afternoon they reached the marina in Tofino where Richard had already made reservations to dock.

***

The weekend was uneventful. Penelope was content that it was so. Most of their time was spent on board partaking of food, wine as well as love making. It had started to rain early Saturday morning so the marina was very quiet. They went further up the coast and Penelope realized that Richard was a very good navigator. She presumed that the course he had taken with the Coast Guard must have been an incentive for him to get to know every aspect of boating. She didn't question him further about his family. Richard on the other hand did not volunteer any more information than the lies he had told her.

What Penelope did not realize was the fact that she was being used by a manipulative con man with no morals, decency or feelings for any-one but himself. His early years in the Middle East had served as a training ground for his future life; he had learned very well. Underneath his camou-flage Benjamin Malouf was not a nice person when things did not go his way or people didn't go along with him. A cold-blooded killer, that's what he really was when being pushed too far.

Penelope was in for some unbelievable surprises!

***

On the top floor of the FBI building on Wilshire Boulevard in West Lost Angeles a meet-ing was taking place in the Office of Gerald Smudgely, Bureau Chief for Southern California. This meeting would eventually have an impact on the lives of some of the residents of the boarding house at 13 Military Street in Victoria, British Co-lumbia, Canada, just a hop from Seattle Washing-ton, USA.

Taking part in the get-together were Chief Inspector Hector Lesage, RCMP (Royal Canadian Mounted Police) headquartered in Ottawa, Cana-da; Sergeant Harry Popleski, RCMP Victoria de-tachment (narcotics); Inspector Alejandro Mar-tinez of Interpol in South America, plus Joan Brent, FBI special undercover agent (Hanna Mueller), as well as Liz Traynor also an FBI spe-cial undercover agent. Both of these ladies were

attached to the narcotics division under the super-
vision of the Southern California Bureau Chief.

Smudgely gave a detailed report of the activities that been noticed by the two ladies after
their two-weeks stay in Victoria, including the
Sunday boat trip. They were not sure if this Captain McMillan was an associate of Benjamin
Malouf or just a hired, hand but that could be
checked locally by the RCMP without arousing
suspicion. The report did mention the close relationship between the suspect and the owner of the
boarding house. It also stated there did not appear
to be a business association of any kind between
the two of them. As a matter of fact the owner's
brother, Sam, had been very helpful when questioned about their family background. These were
ordinary people being manipulated by one of the
best con men alive.

All the participants were very attentive to
what was being said in this high-level security
boardroom.

Inspector Martinez was the first one asked
to report. He told everyone about seeing Gabrielli
Vito in Bogota, Colombia a few months ago. "The
Canadian gangster was going around with well-
known drug cartel members. According to reports
received from agents he appeared to be quite at
ease amongst these associates. They most likely
considered him important in the international family of underworld leaders. Furthermore," Inspector
Martinez added, "Vito had been followed twenty-
four hours a day. He had been seen in good spirits
around Buenaventura, a seaside resort on the coast

of Bogota. We now know," added Martinez, "which of the cartel members your Italian Canadian is dealing with. That information will enable us to inform you rapidly regarding any shipments coming to Canada on any of the drug cartel's 'important' vessels departing for the United States or Canada. I doubt that we'll ever be able to completely stop the drug business. Too much money is involved along with the greed that human beings carry, it becomes a never-ending vicious circle."

Chief Inspector Lesage was next in line to speak. He said he did not have much new information to put on the table except that since the disappearance of one of their informers they had been unsuccessful in finding new "inside information." That was until the day before he left Ottawa to come to Los Angeles. One of his young undercover narcotics officers called him with a request to meet immediately. Officer Delaney out of the Montreal Detachment had befriended a Vito family member by the name of Luciano (known as Lucky) Miranzino a cousin who was not happy with the way Gabby kept things close to his chest by not involving Lucky in the drug business. "This may or may not lead to us having an informer within the close ranks of this criminal family. Since the Lemay incident, Gabby Vito had been very careful about his movements within Canada. At one point, he was supposed to have been in Victoria for a meeting with Malouf but no one even saw a trace of him. He's a cagey one but you can rely on us not giving up our close surveillance, in fact, because of that surveillance we were able to notify Interpol of his going to Bogota. I have six of my best officers assigned to this case. We all feel, and I hope this is the consensus here too, that we should wait for a major shipment if we want to catch the 'Big Boys' involved in this operation."

Bureau Chief Smudgely appreciated all the information that had been given by both visitors. As a final note to the meeting, he passed on the following. "We have been made aware that within a month or two, something big is going to happen with the families involved in the drug business. Our sources out of New York City tell us that the leader of the Syndicate, Leonardo Arminto, who is Vito's uncle, is planning a low-key trip to Montreal or in close proximity of that location. As soon as we can confirm any of this information we'll inform you directly, Chief Inspector. In the meantime let's keep in touch in addition to making sure our surveillance is unrelenting everywhere that it's needed."

The meeting had lasted over three hours and every participant was pleased with the results. Smudgely suggested to Martinez as well as Lesage a dinner for all three. The Brown Derby located at Hollywood and Vine in the heart of Hollywood, where the beautiful people hang out, was an ideal place, he said. It would give the two visitors a look at California's different life style.

They all agreed and parted company until dinnertime for a little personal relaxation.

CHAPTER FIFTEEN…

The boarding house had been very busy with visitors all summer long. The regular guests were reduced by one since Eileen Flowers got married. Reginald Van Orsdal was working hard with his crew of merry men and women getting his play in shape for the forthcoming winter season. They were now rehearsing twice a week in the parlor of the boarding house. The sound of voices in addition to the music added vigor to this otherwise quiet household.

Penelope didn't mind at all, since there were no objections from anyone else, she was rather pleased as the rehearsals created continuous interest without disrupting the generally peaceful atmosphere for the guests.

Since her weekend on the boat with Richard, she had not seen much of him alone as both of them had been rather busy. She was a bit concerned about her brother who was unusually quiet the past couple of weeks. *Yes,* she thought, *since his trip up Island with Jennifer, Sam had kept to himself more than usual. I wonder what's eating him? I must have a talk with him and find out what's wrong, if anything.*

Penelope was sitting at her desk, deep in thoughts, when her brother walked in unexpectedly.

"Hey! Sis, can I talk with you? There's something bothering me and I don't know what to do about it," he said.

"You certainly can, dear brother." Quick thoughts went through her mind that something had gone wrong during his trip with Jennifer. Well, he was just about to tell her anyway, so she stopped thinking about it.

"This really does not have anything to do with my relationship with Jennifer, I want you to know," he went on. "We had a wonderful time together. We got to know each other much better. I must say that she's a marvelous lady, better than anyone I have been associated with in my entire life. Of course, that's always after you, Penelope."

Impatiently, she told him to get to the point and quit beating around the bush.

"I don't know where to begin really but maybe I'm making too much out of this. "Here goes anyway," he said. "After you had left with Richard Taylor, the Friday the two of you went boating, there was a ring at the door. When I answered a tall, athletic-looking man probably in his mid thirties asked to have a private talk with me. Since I didn't know who he was I asked him to identify himself. He showed me a bank ID card, telling me that he was a credit inspector from the Royal Bank. I asked him to follow me to the library and closed the door behind us. I really didn't know what to make of his request."

By this time, Sam really had his sister's undivided attention, she was very anxious to know what this person wanted from her brother. Was it a forgotten debt or what?

Sam went on to say that the man asked him if a Mr. Richard Taylor lived here. "I told him yes, he has for just about a year now." What seemed to be the problem he had asked the bank credit inspector.

"It's not really a problem," the man had replied. "I would thank you for keeping our meeting confidential. You see Mr. Taylor has applied for a rather large business loan. We want to make sure that our investment is safe, you understand?"

He then went on to ask all kinds of questions about his daily habits, who had visited him, how long, how well did we know him? "I had to tell him he was a boarder here that we did not know him prior to his moving in with us. He even asked about your relationship with him. I told him that as far as I knew you only had a casual relationship. Mr. Taylor was a paying guest like all the other people living here. I further added that his business seemed to be doing very well. After I told him that, he thanked me and left. I certainly hope I didn't say too much to hurt his loan application," Sam said. "That's what has been bothering me. Do you think I should mention to Mr. Taylor about the bank inspector's visit?"

"Is that what has been bothering you all this time?" asked Penelope. "My goodness, you should have come to me before. Here I thought it had to do with this nice lady friend of yours. I'm happy that she's not responsible for your strange behavior! Don't let things of this nature bother you, Sam. What people do business-wise is no concern of ours, especially if we're not in a part-nership! I'm glad you told me all this but please, as the man said to you, keep it to yourself. What any of our guests do with their private lives is re-ally none of our concern."

After Sam left the library, Penelope just sat thinking intensely about what her brother had just told her. She remembered times in the past when Jason applied for loans to carry him over a hurdle, as he called it. Bank people would call her with specific questions related to McKee's affairs. In her mind, this was just normal routine with banks, their way of making sure the loan request is legit-imate. She pushed it out of her mind figuring that if Richard wanted her to know how he conducted his business he would tell her so. At that moment the telephone rang. When she answered she was surprised to hear the voice of Hanna Mueller greeting her. "Are you planning to visit us again soon?" Penelope asked.

"Oh no I'm not, but I wish I was," Hanna replied. "The reason I'm calling is that I've mis-placed my camera. I think that I may have left it on the shelf in the closet of that beautiful room on the third floor. Do you think you could check it out for me and call me back? I hate to lose any-thing, especially photos that one can't replace."

"I'll be happy to do that if you give me the number where I can call you, within the half-hour if it's convenient," said Penelope.

She immediately went to the third floor to check on the room Hanna had occupied. As there were no guests occupying any of the rooms at this time there was no need to knock. She entered the room, went directly to the closet, opened the door, could not see anything in her immediate view but as she reached with her hand, felt a strap, grasped it and pulled the camera case from the corner. She figured that Miss Mueller would be happy to find out her camera was safe.

***

What Penelope didn't know was that the photos on the roll had been taken on Taylor's boat as well as inside the warehouse. These were very valuable items for Hanna Mueller and her associates.

Hanna was pleased to hear the good news. She was also relieved the camera was intact. Could she send it by special courier, she would reimburse her for the cost.

"Not a problem," said Penelope. "I look forward to seeing you again whenever you come our way. You're always welcome, as you know, Hanna."

In Los Angeles Hanna thought that she must find a way to make this gentle lady aware of whom Richard Taylor really is. Yet, somehow she had to figure out how to ease the pain that Penelope might suffer before it was too late. She knew what Malouf and his associates were capable of, nothing would stand in their way, or prevent them from reaching their goal. *Yes*, she thought, *I must find a way for this decent person not to be hurt at least not physically hurt.*

***

Late fall came with its winds as well as rainmaking leaving everywhere a very dull depressing time. Fortunately the holiday season was approaching fast. The boarding house had experienced busier days but the calm was welcome now, especially by the kitchen staff. Just looking after the regulars was not so demanding. Nanette needed some time off after a hard working summer and fall.

Penelope was at her desk thinking about the coming Christmas season. She was just remembering the recent wonderful time she had spent going on short trips with Richard either by road or boat. The telephone rang to bring her out of her day-dreaming.

It was Edward at the other end of the line inquiring if he could help putting up the decorations for the holidays. "You know this being the first week of December, it should be done now," he said. "Is Sam around to help me with the work?" he asked.

"I'll make sure he is," said Penelope, "when would you like to come to do all this?" she inquired.

"Tomorrow morning would be fine with me," he replied. "Eileen would like to come over to say hello to everyone. If it's OK with you, Miss Woodspring?"

"It certainly is, Edward," Penelope said with enthusiasm, "I look forward to seeing you both."

***

Richard had been busy leading up to the holiday season with buyers coming to him from all over. He had two hired hands helping with the unloading of shipments from South America and Chile. These two shipments alone had filled 75% of the warehouse space. He still had to unpack his 'special' merchandise alone, which kept him busy until very late in the evening.

He could not take chances with anyone else present. Besides, he had found a place where he could hide some of his special merchandise without anyone ever suspecting where it would be, especially the local RCMP who, for some reason, he suspected was keeping an eye on him. Staying up late in the library of the boarding house had been lucky for him. By pure chance he found the secret passage Penelope had stumbled upon. Richard had read somewhere in a magazine that old Victorian houses, which this boarding house was, often had secret tunnels built at the time of the original construction. The gentlemen of these homes often build an escape tunnel from the library but secret enough that a wife or anyone else could not tell where it was or if they even existed. That way, these 'gentlemen' were able to sneak away undetected for whatever purpose they had in mind. His finding of this great hiding place was pure luck. One evening in early fall he somehow discovered the infamous opening to the secret tunnel by leaning against the wall just behind a big leather chair that was under the stuffed head of a mountain lion.

Fortunately that night, Felicity was out with her man friend. He was able to set things back properly without being discovered. His discovery gave the criminal mind food for thought as well as a reason for testing its safety. He thought that this would be a wonderful place to stash some of his special merchandise until the time came to move it. He would package it properly, place it in a suitcase so that rats or mice could not get to it. The problem might be to bring the suitcase into the boarding house unnoticed.

Richard placed a locking device on the inside of the wall at the maid's quarters end of it so that it would not open from inside Felicity's room. *What a find.* he thought. *I wonder if anyone else in the boarding house knows about this secret passage? I better not question its presence otherwise I won't be able to use it as a hide-away.*

Richard purchased a small steamer trunk all made of metal, which was perfect for what he had in mind. In early December when everyone was busy shopping for Christmas he had the opportunity to sneak his steamer trunk into the library to hide it in the secret tunnel. He made sure it was locked securely so that if found it would not be opened easily.

His contacts had been made with drug runners in Vancouver as well as on the Island. Several runs had already taken place without anyone raising suspicions. He was aware that if he were caught it would be the end of this operation, most probably his own funeral. The Vito crime syndicate would not want to have anyone knowing as much as he did in police custody, with the risk of that person becoming an informer.

For the moment, he pushed those thoughts aside just making sure his runners were doing as they were told. Distributing several hundred pounds of white powder every month was a dangerous task to undertake but also a very profitable one. He had retrieved his briefcase from Penelope's safe in early November, needing some of the cash for his drug dealings.

A few days ago a courier had come all the way from Montreal by way of New Foundland, New Brunswick, Toronto, Winnipeg and finally Vancouver where he had boarded a ferry to Nanaimo to meet with Richard.

This contact man had a special sealed envelope for Richard. He was to return to Toronto from Vancouver within a day or two.

When Richard returned from Nanaimo he went directly to his warehouse office to open this important envelope! The letter inside was in Italian and French. It contained information for him to meet a fishing boat in the Queen Charlotte Islands possibly in mid-March of next year, as well as making sure to have with him two hundred 2 kilos bags of the white powder. This merchandise was to be turned over to these 'fishermen'. They were identified with a code number that he would decipher later on.

These individuals were big drug barons from New York. They would be in Seattle for some days prior to their fishing trip in Alaska. One of them was Pietro Arminto, the son of Don Leonardo, uncle of Gabby Vito. Nothing else needs to be added in this regard. Richard was fully aware that he could not afford anything to go wrong. After thinking about his plan, he realized he would need to hire Captain McMillan for the special fishing trip. Since the trip was far up the coast of BC he preferred to have someone who knew how to navigate in these strange waters. Letting Captain McMillan know in late February about the planned trip would be sufficient time for him to chart the best route to navigate. His next thought was whether or not to take Penelope along as an added cover-up. There was sufficient time ahead of him before making a final decision.

***

The Christmas festivities of the boarding house started around the 20th of December. They did not end until the first Monday in January.

1957 was going to be a special year according to Reginald Van Orsdal's predictions. He was fortunate at having secured a theater in downtown Victoria from the third week of January to the end of March, assuming his play was still going strong. Van Orsdal knew his group was ready to perform for the public. He advertised *'What Maddened the Gods,'* as the sure-fire remedy for the winter blues. "A good laugh," he said "will put your spirits back on the right path in addition to drive away your feelings of depression."

Everyone at the boarding house was looking forward to opening night scheduled for the third Saturday in January. Richard Taylor had been so kind as to purchase two dozen tickets which he gave to the regular boarders as well as his business clientele. The cost didn't matter to him he would use it as a business expense.

Because of the busy holiday season Penelope and Richard had not had a chance to go away together. One night after everyone had left the dining room Richard told Penelope that he was planning a boat trip to Seattle around the end of January. Would she like to come along for two or three days? Just the two of them, it would be a wonderful short vacation away from the daily pressures business places you under.

"Well," she answered, "it will probably set the year off in the right direction. I wouldn't think of missing such a chance at getting away from it all. A boat trip is just what the doctor ordered. Since this is a slow time of the year for both our businesses we could extend the time by a day or two. That is, if you can do that, Richard?"

"I think that it can be arranged," he said.

With that in mind they parted company for the evening.

For once she would be able to give Felicity and her brother some advance notice. In her mind she was already looking forward to a few days of great exhilaration. On her way from the dining room she stopped in the kitchen to inform

Felicity about her forthcoming trip. Would she be able to look after the place in her absence once again?

"As always," said Felicity, "it'll be a pleasure to take care of business for you, dear friend."

***

Chief Inspector Hector Lesage had received instructions from his superiors to send to Victoria newly promoted Inspector Michael J. Woodchuck. The Inspector had spent the last five years working directly with Scotland Yard and Interpol in England. In the memo Lesage received, Woodchuck was described as a Canadian Citizen born in England with fourteen years of Police experience.

This January morning Lesage was waiting in his office for the arrival of Inspector Woodchuck. He wished to bring him up to date on the special investigation ongoing in Victoria British Columbia. Lesage had also called in Sergeant Popleski to be there to meet his new boss at the same time. New developments had occurred since the last meeting in Los Angeles. The Chief Inspector wanted his team members to be up-dated.

Officer Delaney had succeeded in strengthening his relationship with Lucky Miranzino. Some startling information had been passed on that could be crucial to the success of this major operation. It had been code named 'Oceanside' to separate it from other investigations of less importance.

After introductions were made, an up-date to the investigation for the benefit of the new team member was presented in detail without interruptions. Chief Inspector

Lesage told his two colleagues that the information he was about to give them was crucial to the success of their endeavor, which was, of course, the arrest of Benjamin Malouf (a.k.a. Richard Taylor) and possibly members of the Vito crime family. He went on to say that he had not yet informed his American counterpart. "You two are the first to know about Officer Delaney's success in gaining inside information on the Vitriolli family. Along with that is the possible acquisition of a new informer.

"We have it from confirmed sources that sometime in late March or April of this year, a big deal or exchange is going to happen somewhere on the Northern Coast of BC. Possibly in the vicinity of the Queen Charlotte Islands. That tells us boats will be involved. Since we know that Malouf bought a 36-foot cruiser with two diesel engines last year, the probability of him being directly involved is considerable. The question is; who is the other party? So far all we know is some big shot from New York will be in the group. Possibly someone from the Arminto crime family. For that reason alone I have to inform my American counterpart quickly."

"The coastal waters of British Columbia cover too great a distance to be covered by a single patrol vessel. We need to have better information as to the place of their rendezvous. I know we can get the Coast Guard to help us at any time but, the fewer people know about this, the better chance we have of succeeding. It would not be a bad idea to keep an eye on the daily activities of Richard Taylor. I understand he takes quite a few weekend excursions in his 'toy-boat' including a lady friend with him.

"A tighter surveillance of Taylor's movements is in order at this time. Remember that we can't take the risk of being spotted. We need a very soft approach with this individual. He's a professional smuggler with widespread experience. This is where you'll be a great asset to the team, Inspector Woodchuck. I understand you were a Naval officer at one time, does that mean you have fairly good knowledge of boats?"

"You're right, Sir," said the tall and thick bushy-haired former Englishman who still had an English accent. "My experience in dealing with smugglers anywhere in the world makes me realize they're all greedy and very dangerous. I have carefully studied the file of this Taylor chap. From what I can see we'll have to be especially careful with him. He was trained by the best, in Lebanon. In my early days of serving with Interpol, I was one of the lucky ones who did not get blown up by his father. They first train their people in the art of terrorism. Then show them how to silently kill a person. This is followed by how to be successful smuggling through any type of obstacle, border or terrain, by water, land or air.

Yes, Chief Inspector, this kind of man is not to be taken lightly at any time. We never did

capture his father. He along with three other associates was gunned down in a battle with law enforcement officers in the small community of San
Remo Italy, near the French border. Nine other
people died in that shoot-out, seven of them were
civilians that Malouf Senior had taken hostage."

Then on a less serious vein he went on to
say, "I don't know very much about motor boats
but at one time I owned a forty-foot sailboat. To
control that baby you had to be proficient in the
art of sailing."

"We should continue our surveillance and
get back together, by the end of February or early
March. Presumably once you speak with your
American counterparts you may have additional
information for us. Let's stay in close contact."

***

Opening night was three days away, which
made Reginald Van Orsdal very nervous. Not
about the sale of tickets since he had a sold-out
performance but more about how the 'reserved'
people of Victoria would react to such a crazy
play. People were very conservative in their ways
in this old British colony. Especially so when it
came to their involvement in the arts.

Joyce Mahoney, on the other hand, was
quite up-beat about the whole thing. To her, in
some ways, it was a return to her saloon performing days. She had purchased a new outfit on the
advice of the Professor. Since he had been involved in teaching the arts for so many years, she
trusted his judgment.

Everyone from the boarding house was at the theater, as well as Eileen and her husband Edward who now lived in Oak Bay with the more sedate population.

From the applause together with the laughter from the audience, Reginald knew his play was a success. This brought tears to his eyes. After so many years of waiting with very little hope of success in sight, he finally gained some recognition. When it was over, the whole theater stood up and applauded for at least seven or eight minutes. A standing ovation to be remembered by the actors who were introduced one by one by the proud Van Orsdal himself.

The Professor knew that some art critics were in the audience. He would look forward to their comments in the paper as well as on the local radio the next day.

After the play, several members of the audience came backstage to personally congratulate the cast. Reginald Van Orsdal was a happy man.

Penelope invited the whole cast back to the boarding house for refreshments. Felicity had ordered hors d'oeuvres and other goodies from Jean-François's catering. Richard Taylor had brought in a case of wine as well as a few bottles of champagne.

The party lasted well after two in the morning. Since Sam was the only sober one, he volunteered to drive people home.

The following morning almost everyone was late for breakfast as some were showing signs of a hangover. Van Orsdal had a difficult time to find words of appreciation for everything as well as everyone, especially for Penelope, that "classy lady" as he referred to her.

In the opinion of the arts connoisseurs locally and province wide, the play was what it purported to be, "A remedy for the winter blues." Because of favorable critiques, advance tickets sold quickly. So much so, that the theater was sold out completely to the end of March. Van Orsdal and his group of 'wannabes' were on cloud nine, deservedly so!

***

Richard was still in his bathrobe preparing his small suitcase for the boat trip with Penelope, when the telephone rang. "Taylor here," he answered! A familiar voice told him that there were some changes in the up-coming fishing trip, would he call back for details, nothing urgent but when he had a free moment.

He first finished his morning ablutions and his packing, then went to the dining room for breakfast where he informed Penelope that he had an errand to run before they departed.

She was sitting alone lingering over coffee when Richard came in the dining room; he informed her that they would leave a half-hour later than previously arranged because of a small business matter he had to take care of.

When he returned Gabby's call he was informed that everything was fine except that his Uncle Vincent Vitriolli had decided to come along on the fishing trip. "Furthermore," he said, "Uncle Leonardo who's married to Uncle Vincent's sister has also decided to be with the party. As you can see, Richard, most of the crime controlling families of North America will be collected together for the first time. We have to make sure the trip goes well without attracting attention from any source either journalistic or law enforcement."

Richard realized immediately the importance this forthcoming trip had taken. After thanking Gabby for the information, he assured him all would be well. He told him how he was proposing to get to the rendezvous point. These northern BC waters were too much of a challenge for him. He would hire Captain McMillan, the old sea dog, to navigate for him. That way Richard said it will be safer all around. "I'll only have to be concerned with my 'gifts' for the visitors. The Captain will not have the opportunity to meet any of the 'uncles'. I'll make sure of that."

Gabby Vito said that he was satisfied with Richard's plans. He somehow would be in touch again a week or two prior to the fishing trip.

Richard returned to the boarding house feeling better about the whole thing. Previous telephone calls had placed a doubt in his mind until the air was cleared. He did not feel a hundred percent comfortable about receiving early morning calls from Gabby Vito.

Back at the boarding house he told Penelope that everything was in order. He was ready to go if she was.

"I certainly am," she replied picking-up her bag.

***

When they arrived at the boat moorage, Richard said that it would take him a few minutes to review the charts to make sure they would be sailing on the right course. His radio equipment was turned on, he started the engine and they were on their way for a fabulous short vacation, just the two of them.

For Penelope going away with Richard was a useful therapy that helped her get over the past. This trip was going to be more of an adventure as well as a fact-finding trip; she had never been to Seattle by sea. It would take about four hours to get there. The weather was co-operative making the trip very relaxing.

After arriving at the marina, Richard told Penelope he had to make a quick call after clearing Customs to correct something he had forgotten to tell his warehouse staff.

What he did not say to her was that he had to contact the man in charge of all drug deliveries for the Arminto family. Aboard his yacht he had hidden one hundred and sixty packages of two kilos each ready to be turned over for breakdown and street distribution.

Richard had arranged the cabin of his boat in such a way that he was able to remove the wall paneling, hide all of his 'special merchandise,' then replace the paneling.

While he and Penelope were playing tourist in Seattle for four hours or so, the 'client' would be visiting the yacht, removing the merchandise, leaving payment, replacing the wall paneling without a trace.

Very clever this Richard was! By doing it this way, he had eliminated several 'runners' along with the risk of being caught. How often he could do this, he didn't know. But, he was sure that if he prepared himself well for the forthcoming trip to the Queen Charlottes, he would be very successful. He still had to figure out what to do with Captain McMillan and Penelope if he decided to take her on the trip. That would come to him in due course, he was sure of it.

***

They had dinner in one of Seattle's finest restaurant. At one point Richard went to the washroom, made a telephone call, was informed that the operation had gone well. Now he could really relax as well as enjoy the next three or four days if the weather co-operated.

CHAPTER SIXTEEN...

Mid-February is the beginning of spring in Victoria, a wonderful time. Trees are starting to bud and flowers are blooming in many places. The boarding house had been a busy place since the opening of Reginald Van Orsdal's play. It had really taken off, becoming a box office success. The play had the ingredients necessary to cheer-up a conservative Victoria theater crowd. After each performance, the whole cast gathered in the parlor at the boarding house. They appreciated the standing invitation given to them by Penelope on opening night. It was like a cooling down time after a big run.

Felicity would prepare snacks with substance as she called them, for the hungry ones who had been on stage almost three hours.

To keep the festive atmosphere, Joyce would bang a few notes on the old upright piano. singing tunes from her days in the Yukon. Everyone had a good time. Penelope just accepted that her family had increased for the moment. Keeping herself busy and distracted from thoughts of Richard Taylor was a needed exercise for her, because she didn't want to be fully committed. She wanted to leave her options open. Although Richard had told her some of his family history, there was still something nagging at the back of her mind. Was it intuition or was it just extra sensory perception that was warning her to be careful, to go easy with this relationship?

***

The end of March arrived too quickly. It was not surprising that Reginald Van Orsdal's play had box office support to keep going for four more weeks.

There had not been many newcomers at the boarding house, except of course for the theater group which kept the place hopping. Reginald was so pleased with his performers that he was already planning to have another one for next year. He had made enough money to pay every cast member handsomely, as well as his expenses, rental of the theater and still have a substantial amount left in the bank. *Yes indeed,* he thought, *Victoria was a theater going-city!*

***

Richard Taylor was suffering growing pains, business-wise that is. His imports from the world over were in great demand. He had expanded his business to major cities in Alberta and as far east as Montreal.

The catalogue he had prepared to be distributed across North America was now bringing in orders from different cities everywhere. He had so much business that he was forced to hire a sales person along with a receptionist to handle the large number of telephone calls that were steadily coming in. This, in itself, was useful because it took away the need to ever have to justify the large quantity of imports from China, South America, Chile, including India arriving by ships on a regular basis. In a way it also helped to camouflage the illegal side of his imports. This made it easier for him to move the drugs received from the Colombian cartel.

The constant fear of possibly being watched bothered him a bit. He couldn't be sure that he was under non-stop surveillance but didn't want to discuss it with Gabby who would probably send Gino, the terminator, to keep an eye on things.

Richard was not favorable to having this kind of individual around for any period of time. People would really get suspicious then. Besides, he had to prepare for his intended important trip to the Queen Charlottes. Since his trip to Seattle with Penelope, he had been able to do three more. For those trips he hired Captain McMillan to handle the navigation. He was busy with clients as guests for an evening in Seattle. These clients were local storeowners that purchased Richard's imports on a regular basis. On each trip he had taken fifty packages of his 'special merchandise' in the same manner as before, by hiding the packages behind the wall paneling inside the cabin. Because of the high volume of his business, he was able to move large amounts of cash in various directions to different bank accounts within Canada as well as offshore.

The captain didn't even suspect that Taylor was having him move large quantities of cocaine across the border.

*** voila

Inspector Michael Woodchuck was planning a surprise for Richard Taylor. He and his men had him under surveillance practically twenty-four hours a day. They had succeeded in planting one of their people as a warehouse helper. They thought an undercover agent would be able to find badly needed information. They knew how tight-lipped Taylor was, but patience was on their side.

One thing the Inspector did not expect, was the lucky break that Taylor got. After working three weeks as a laborer in the warehouse, the undercover agent got himself in an argument with the senior warehouse helper. The argument heated up one day to end in a fistfight. Once Taylor found out what the argument was about, who started it, he fired the undercover agent on the spot. Inspector Woodchuck was not too pleased with the situation. He released the officer to regular duties in the Vancouver area.

In the meantime, the regular warehouse man brought in a friend who was immediately hired by Taylor. Luck was really on this smuggler's side. No one had been able to catch him at doing anything illegal, not even a speeding ticket!

Yes, Taylor had been well trained. He most likely had more patience as well as street smarts than many of the young police officers assigned to watch over him. His international experience gave him the edge he needed to meet any unexpected challenge, no matter how big.

There might be one exception to Taylor's edge in the arrival of Inspector Michael Woodchuck who had also been trained by the best in his field.

Since arriving in Victoria, the Inspector had several meetings with the Commander of the Canadian Coast Guard. He was able to obtain the use of a boat from him providing he used one of the Coast Guard pilots. Woodchuck had no problem agreeing with that request. He made sure the pilot would understand the nature of the RCMP's work at sea plus the danger it entailed. By being flexible the Inspector was able to have the Coast Guard unit train a couple of constables to be assigned extra sea patrol duties since this Coast Guard cutter was ocean ready. In the long run, the Inspector knew his international experience as well as his patience would eventually pay off.

***

Sitting across from his sister who was obviously deep in thought, Sam was finishing his breakfast. He had to call her name three times before she responded.

"Yes, Sam," she said, "what is it? I'm sorry, my thoughts were just floating in outer space, I guess."

"Well," said Sam, "next Saturday is Jennifer's birthday. I was wondering if it would be OK for me to have a little birthday party for her right here in our home?"

"It don't see why not, Sam," she replied. "As a matter of fact I think that the following day is Felicity's birthday. Maybe we could have a 'double party' if that's agreeable with you?"

"I'm sure it would be just wonderful," Sam smiled. "That way Jennifer would not feel so self-conscious. It's a marvelous idea, Penelope, but how are we going to arrange the food serving if Felicity is in the party?"

"Not a problem Sam, I'll have Jean-François's catering do the dinner that night. Will that take care of everything for the moment?"

"I would like to pay for half of the cost then, if you don't mind," Sam said.

Penelope was really happy that she could do something nice for her brother, (he deserved a little happiness she thought!) She told him that she would pay his half and Felicity's birthday present from both of us will be the other half.

After Sam left the dining room she just sat at the table, thinking back to her latest trip with Richard. What a delightful three days that had been, just the two of them exploring, fishing and basically just doing nothing but being together. She realized he was not the talkative kind, that made her wonder a bit, but it was fine with her. She had decided not to question him anymore unless he started to talk about his family background or childhood again. However, she still had this nagging feeling in her mind that warned her to be careful about her relationship with Richard Taylor. *Maybe if I go away alone somewhere for a week or two, I might find out how I really feel about this man. Now here's a thought worth going after.*

Richard had mentioned he would be going away for a week or ten days in early or mid-April to see a very important client who would possibly bring some new business from New York. A fishing trip was in order if that's what it took to open up the American markets, he had said.

Richard had told her he would leave the charting of the destination to Captain McMillan, an old hand at navigating coastal waters.

Perhaps, she thought, this would be the perfect time for her to take a vacation on her own, maybe in sunny California.

Penelope remembered that Hanna Mueller, in a conversation, had given her a standing offer to come down to Southern California for a visit, as long as she could let her know ahead of time so not to interfere with her being away on location, filming somewhere. *Yes,* she thought, *the more I think of it, the more I like it. I just won't tell anyone yet.*

She went to the library where her office was located and made a call to Hanna Mueller in Los Angeles. Hannah was somewhat surprised to hear from Penelope, but at the same time happy that this occasion might give her the chance to explain to that wonderful lady how dangerous this Richard Taylor was. Of course, she would have to be very diplomatic about the whole thing so as not to interfere with the investigation that was ongoing, worldwide, centered on Taylor and his associates.

The conversation was fairly short. Penelope did not have the exact date yet. One week away from it all was what she needed before going on a two-week fishing trip that Richard had mentioned. She was just checking to see if the offer was still open expecting to arrange her schedule to fit Hanna's.

She no sooner put the telephone down that it rang, she picked it up surprised to hear Richard's voice.

He wanted to inform her that they would be leaving in three weeks for the fishing trip. They would most likely be gone twelve to fourteen days. Going to the Queen Charlotte Islands, he said, would certainly be quite an adventure. Before leaving he needed to get his briefcase from her safe. Would she be there around noon hour, he asked?

Penelope told him that she would be home all-day. "Come in and let me know when you would want the safe opened," she said.

At noon Richard arrived and decided to stay for lunch. It was unusual for him to be away from his business at noontime. After lunch he retrieved his briefcase from the safe. He told Penelope that he was just going to his room for a few minutes to get something. Taylor said he would be back to replace the briefcase in the safe momentarily.

While in his room he wrote a short letter addressed to Penelope. In his message Richard told her that if ever anything happened to him, she was to keep for herself the small box that he was returning to the safe. Make sure that you don't divulge the contents to anyone. He also advised her not to take it to the bank as someone might question where she got such a large sum of money. The reasons, he said, are unimportant, as there would be a tremendous amount of news information that would make her understand his decision to do this.

Richard took all of the Canadian cash from the briefcase placing one hundred and fifty thousand dollars in a small cardboard box. After sealing it he fastened the letter on top with a rubber band. He kept fifty thousand Canadian dollars plus what was left of the American cash.

Penelope was waiting for him in the library. When he came in, she opened the safe door again but noticed that instead of replacing the briefcase in the safe, he placed a small box he was carrying in his hands. She didn't say anything as she observed him place the box on a shelf. Richard placed it on its side to prevent the address on the envelope from being in full view as you opened the safe doors.

Seeing the inquisitive look on her face, Richard told her that he was just going to leave some valuables in the safe, needing to take his briefcase with him. He gave her a hug, a kiss and left to return to his warehouse where he had a lot to do to prepare for the 'fishing trip'.

After locking the safe, Penelope called the airport to make a reservation for her trip to Los Angeles. She decided to leave in three days in order to be back on time for the fishing trip with

Richard. She then called Hanna again to inform her what she was about to do. Penelope wanted to know if it would be all right with her to come to Los Angeles right now. She went on to say that she and Richard were leaving on a fourteen-day fishing trip somewhere in the Queen Charlotte Islands. He was going there to meet with a group of business clients from New York. She needed to get away from here to possibly talk with someone whom she could trust. "You see, Hanna, there are some things that are unsure in my mind when it comes to my relationship with Richard Taylor. There's something nagging at me that I can't put my finger on."

Hanna replied for her to get down here, assuring her a relaxing time. "We'll talk about everything and nothing when you get here Penelope. I shall look forward to picking you up at the airport in three days."

"By the way," Penelope added, "only my brother Sam and Felicity will know about my trip. I would rather keep it quiet, that way I don't have to answer questions from the other boarders."

Hanna could not believe her ears. What a piece of luck! She immediately called Bureau Chief Gerald Smudgely and requested an urgent meeting. Maybe things were finally looking up for a change as she knew that no one had been able to get further information concerning the 'big deal' which was to happen in March or April. "Thank you, Penelope," she mused. "Thank you so very much."

***

The birthday party for Felicity and Jennifer was a great success. Jean-François's catering did the whole thing. All the boarders were invited, Eileen and her husband Edward as well. Penelope had also included Nanette on the party list. All together it was a delightful evening with a lot of bonhomie. Sam had a permanent smile on his face that evening. It was obvious to his sister that he was head over heels in love. *If only that could happen to me*, she thought.

She had read somewhere that one's destiny is decided at a very early age. Not that she believed much of this astrological philosophy but it would be nice to know. She had seen in small ads of the local paper that Palm Readers could tell you the future for two dollars. They would give you a whole half-hour of predictions on love as well as business for five dollars. She wondered how much of that stuff was true or how much was just plain nonsense.

Years ago a girlfriend had told her she had her palm read. Just about everything that was foretold to her did happen. The more she thought about this astrological phenomena, card readers and palm readers, the more she convinced herself that she should, at least, try it.

***

The Bureau Chief told agent Brent to take some time off to take good care of her guest and maybe acquire even more information if at all possible.

***

Penelope arrived in Los Angeles in late afternoon. She found the temperature to be suffocating. Ninety-two degrees Fahrenheit, the pilot informed the passengers before landing. Just as she walked through the terminal she saw Hanna's cheerful face looking directly at her.

After a hug and greetings, they went to the carrousel to pick up her suitcase. She had brought one piece of luggage, knowing that she could only stay a week in the warmth of Southern California. They arranged for a porter to load up the luggage in the trunk of the Cadillac.

Hanna drove through part of downtown Los Angeles to the 101 Freeway, also known as the Hollywood Freeway and then North to Toluca Lake where she had a lovely fully-fenced one and a half-acre property. The swimming pool was quite colorful surrounded by chairs, tables, umbrellas etc. The house had five bedrooms on the second story. The downstairs quarters were designed for entertaining with its large dining room and living room. There was seven thousand square feet of living space all decorated with feminine charm. Hanna had two dogs and two cats. To help with all this, she had a live-in maid from South America, who pretended that she could hardly speak English.

Penelope was not surprised at the comfort in Hanna's residence. What would surprise her were the conversations she was going to have with her host. The lady from Victoria was in for a real awakening.

***

Shortly after Chief Inspector Lesage completed his phone call with Gerald Smudgely of the FBI in Los Angeles, his secretary informed him that Constable Delaney had called from Montreal saying that it was urgent for the Chief Inspector to call back.

When Delaney came on the line, he told his superior that he had some information that was, without a doubt, vital to the success of operation "Oceanside." Could he come to Ottawa immediately to discuss it with him together with other members of the narcotics team working on this project. He told the Chief Inspector he could be there in about two and a half-hours.

After listening to Constable Delaney, Chief Inspector Lesage told him to come as quickly as possible. He would arrange for other members of the team to be present.

Once they were all together Delaney told his story from the beginning. He started at the time when he was only having a simple conversation with Luciano (Lucky) Miranzino, who was actually a nephew of Vincent Vitriolli therefore, a cousin to Gabrielli Vito the actual enforcer of the crime family. Although Vincent was 'retired,' he was still the 'don' or godfather of this highly organized crime syndicate. Lucky, as he was known, was not as close to his cousin Gabby as he would have liked to be.

Miranzino had a drinking problem and was known to be very cruel to women partners. These traits, according to rumors circulating in the crime circles of Montreal, made him likely to open his mouth too easily. But since he was family, it was said that Gabby just kept him on the payroll. Officer Delaney went on to say that Lucky Miranzino was smart enough to know there were important things happening in the family. For some reason he was being kept out of the loop. He was afraid to confront Gabby, knowing that he would not hesitate to put out a "contract" on him using Gino "the eliminator" to carry it out. One day when he was at the Vito's house, he overheard a conversation that Gabby was having on the telephone with someone in British Columbia. He heard him say that the fishing trip was planned for April 20th and that Uncle Vincent would join Uncle Leonardo on the trip. Lucky did not know exactly where this trip was taking place but knew that most likely Benji Malouf (Taylor) would be coming up from Victoria with gifts for the uncles.

"As I had done before, Inspector," Delaney said, "I didn't question him but rather just let him vent his frustrations." This overheard conversation was not necessarily confirmation that a "'Godfather meeting' was about to take place. The fact that it was not said in front of Lucky directly but rather overheard by him, seemed to be one important indicator that round the clock surveillance should be placed on Taylor immediately. Delaney went on, "That way we can watch every move he makes. I really think, Sir, that this information is accurate. I've been dealing with the Vito family for two years now. I know that Gabby bypasses his cousin on many occasions. To keep him out of their hair, they gave him one of the Montreal downtown nightclubs to operate.

"By doing that, Gabby had kept cousin Luciano out of the drug business because I believe he doesn't trust him. There may come a day when Lucky disappears like Lemay did some months ago, I wouldn't be at all surprised!"

"Well," the Chief Inspector said, "we finally have some substantive information. With the additional information I got today from Bureau Chief Smudgely of the FBI, it all fits together. Miss Woodspring, the owner of the boarding house, where Taylor lives in Victoria, will be flying to Los Angeles in a day or two. She told one of Smudgely's agents that she and Taylor were going on a two-week fishing trip up the BC coast to the Queen Charlotte Islands. For your information I've been in touch with Inspector Woodchuck in Victoria who also informed me they were aware Taylor was preparing for some kind of trip. His men were watching every move he was making. Unfortunately what they didn't know and it would not be easy to find out was who the participants to the trip were, as well as the exact location of the meeting in the Queen Charlottes. Your information is very valuable to operation 'Oceanside', Constable Delaney," Lesage said. "I must say that you've done a fantastic job.

"Any updates or changes in our information must be shared immediately. If we hope, or should I say, if we intend, to apprehend this group of international drug smugglers, we have not only to co-ordinate our efforts and information as quickly as possible but place everything else aside to make operation 'Oceanside' our top priority for the time being.

"Does anyone have any other comments?" Lesage asked. "Thank you all for coming, lets keep each other informed no matter how trivial we may think the matter is. It could be that a small lure will land the big fish."

Once his men had left, Lesage immediately called Woodchuck in Victoria to inform him of the new developments about Malouf (Taylor) and the Vito family. During the conversation, Inspector Woodchuck told his superior they had succeeded in getting an excellent undercover man close to Malouf. So far it had proven to be their best move. They were all aware he was moving 'special merchandise' but had not found how he was doing it yet.

Hector Lesage picked-up the telephone again to dial Smudgely's private line number in Los Angeles. After three rings, a voice came on, "Smudgely here."

"Its Lesage in Ottawa, my friend. I have some news that will undoubtedly confirm what you've been telling me." The Chief Inspector went on to give him details of the meeting he just had with Constable Delaney and his team.

The Bureau Chief was delighted with this information, especially since it seemed to coincide with the reports he was getting from his field operatives. "We're going to put a tail on Mr. Arminto. We should be able to pin-point where he's going including with whom to the West

Coast. I do believe that we'll have to get our people to work close together on this case. This information now appears to be getting more and
more interesting. Is your Inspector in Victoria up
to date on all this?" asked Smudgely.

"He certainly is," said Lesage. "Furthermore he has succeeded in placing a former lieu-
tenant, who is now retired, as an informer working
side by side with Malouf. We know that he hides
the drugs in his warehouse but we don't know as
yet, how it's packaged or how he moves it from
the warehouse to the runners for distribution."

"This is very interesting," Smudgely said,
"but are you absolutely confident about your 'informer'? Is he aware how dangerous this individual is? You know that he would slit his throat with
one hand while eating his sandwich with the other.
This would not disturb Malouf one bit, if he had
any suspicions as to your man's real identity."

The Chief Inspector reassured him that
McMillan was an old hand at dealing with dangerous criminals. "During his days with the force,
he was the best actor the RCMP ever had. Nine
years ago, after his wife died in a small plane
crash in Alberta, he took a retirement package. He
decided to become a real expert on the coastal waters of British Columbia. McMillan undertook
several marine training courses, earned a coastal
Pilot's ticket. He also did a special study on the
waters, straits and inlets from Mexico to Alaska.
This man has the knowledge of a captain with
twenty years of sea-going experience. Furthermore, if there is any sensitive information to be

found, old Tom will find it. He just has a nose for things out of the ordinary.

"If I were a betting man, I'd put my money on McMillan to come out on top in any difficult or dangerous situation. Believe me, Smudgely, said Lesage, "there isn't a better man around!"

They promised to keep one another informed on all changes related to this very sensitive investigation. Their goal was to apprehend the heads of the two largest crime families in North America.

***

In Los Angeles Penelope was having a very restful time enjoying the sunshine at the backyard swimming pool. Nothing like total peace and relaxation to rebuild one's energies. She was doing some deep thinking, and more importantly, sorting out her feelings concerning her relationship with Richard Taylor. There were certain things he had done which she did not feel comfortable about. For instance, one time he said he was going to Nanaimo on business. By chance she saw him going into a downtown restaurant with two 'unsavory looking' individuals. His many boat trips to Seattle with business clients made her wonder about their true intent. She further questioned the many visits he received from shady individuals at the guesthouse. Since he was a paying guest, partly because she wanted her relationship to be casual, she kept these thoughts to herself. However, away from it all she was just going over the events from the time he moved in as a guest. Penelope remembered that Felicity warned her a few times but never did say anything definite. She also recollected the time her brother informed her of the 'bank inspector's visit' inquiring about Richard Taylor. She had checked with the bank to be told they would never send an employee of the bank to verify someone's credit abilities. This was always done by telephone, she was reassured.

She also had questions about what was in that briefcase he had placed in the safe at one time. She remembered about the boat he had pur-chased, in cash as he had told her. Richard had never told her where he went to school, if he had brothers and sisters, if he went to university. All the usual things that a normal person talks about. He never talked about sports that he either played or liked to watch. Most men in Canada are either hockey or football fans or both. With Richard the-se subjects never came up in a conversation. Now that she was away from her domestic scene, she was able to think more clearly realizing that Rich-ard Taylor purposely avoided all subjects related to his past. A question popped to her mind, "Who is this Richard Taylor?"

***

The maid came to the pool area to inform her lunch was ready. Would she come to join her host? She automatically got up, walking towards the dining room but kept on thinking about her relationship with Richard Taylor. *I'll have to think*

about this some more. I've got to find some an-
swers to put my mind at ease.

"Well," exclaimed Hanna, "you look like the cat that swallowed the canary, dear friend. Let's have a light lunch then we can take a trip to Palm Springs, if you'd like."

Penelope was quite agreeable to any suggestions that Hanna might make. She needed someone to take charge so she wouldn't have to think about anything including her private life. "I haven't been here twenty-four hours, I already feel this environment becoming so soothing," said Penelope. "There are some things I would like to talk over with you at some point. First I have to get them straight in my head to make sure I'm not going off on a tangent. I want to be honest with myself in addition to being just as honest with you."

"Whatever you would like to discuss with me will be between the two of us, I assure you of that," said Hanna, "furthermore if I can, I'll be glad to help in whatever way possible."

Everyone in Hanna's circle of friends knew who she was, including what she did for a living. She had informed them she was bringing a new friend who, for the time being, only knew her as Hanna Mueller. Since most of her friends were also FBI agents she thought that maintaining her cover at being Hanna Mueller would be an easier task for the moment. She had not considered Penelope's perception that was at its keenest in times of personal turmoil.

Hanna knew that once Penelope confided in her, she would have to disclose her true identity. Penelope was no fool, she had worked with one of the world's best-known reporters as his executive assistant for nearly fifteen years, also traveled the globe with him. Her knowledge as well as her assessment of people had to be better than the average person.

Well, I'll just have to play it by ear and weigh every word. With such high stakes, caution was the key here.

It appeared to this compassionate FBI agent that Penelope Woodspring whilst on a soul searching mission was about to discover life's cruel reality.

CHAPTER SEVENTEEN...

Penelope and Hanna were sitting by the pool enjoying a glass of wine and getting to know each other better. They had spent the last five or six days doing the tourist trap at Disneyland including going down to the Mission in San Juan Capistrano, plus a trip to the famous San Diego Zoo.

"I'm having a wonderful time," Penelope began, "but there are a few things on my mind that I would like to talk over with you, although perhaps I should go to a psychiatrist," she said tongue in cheek!

That brought a chuckle from Hanna who added, "Thanks for the compliment."

"I'm very serious," Penelope said. "For months now I have had the feeling that something's going on at my boarding house. Does that make any sense to you, Hanna?"

"I don't exactly know what you want to tell me but go ahead," she replied. "I'm a good listener, I promise to be quite straightforward with any comments I may have later."

Penelope started her story. "I've been thinking about this for some time now. Let me go back to the time Richard Taylor rented my last available room in the guesthouse. Since that time, it seems to me that several strangers from across Canada as well as the United States, including yourself, have been visiting Victoria. My relationship with Richard Taylor started as a casual acquaintance and developed into a love affair. But I haven't and will not make any serious commitment at this point. You may or may not know that prior to my moving to Victoria I had an ongoing relationship of some fifteen years of duration. It was mostly happy times with the man who left the house to me. He died when we were on holidays in Cuba. It was a shock to me. I'm still having a difficult time putting it all behind me. After traveling all over the world with a companion for that length of time, you just can't throw it away overnight you know.

"When Richard Taylor showed up at the front door of the boarding house, I thought I was seeing a ghost. His physical resemblance to Jason McKee was so close that, for a moment, I was stunned. He was such a smooth talker with the right words at the right time, just as if he knew what I wanted to hear. That part of his personality bothered me but as you know, we as women, like to be flattered as well as pampered in some way. It's good for our self-esteem. In the beginning, the few times that he asked me to accompany him, he was a bit distant, not pushy or anxious like most single middle-aged men would be. He didn't even make a pass at me. That also, raised some questions in my head but I figured that sooner or later I would find out what made him tick."

"It took a few months before he invited me to spend the weekend with him Up Island. As I said I was in no hurry to start a relationship anyway. I thought that the weekend away would be an opportunity to get to know him better to find out about his background. How wrong I was! Richard Taylor was very evasive about his family, only told me that his mother and father had died in a car accident. Somehow he always found a way to avoid my direct questions. Since my concerns for his feelings were always much on my mind, I would not allow myself to pursue any conversation that Richard did not want to get into.

"What increased my concerns were things that might not be on the up and up with Richard. Every time we went on a boat trip either up Island or towards Seattle, he was always concerned, or appeared to be, about anyone following us or watching us. I sensed that there was something he was hiding, but I didn't like to ask questions. Everywhere we stopped he always had to make a telephone call about an urgent matter he had forgotten or a message he had to give a client. For a man who appeared to project such a competent business demeanor, I found his behavior a bit suspicious. Not that I have a suspicious mind, but it disturbed me that he would do these things every time we went on a trip. One thing right from the beginning, which concerned me and still does today, was the large amounts of money he would have on hand after every trip.

"There was this one trip he made on his own to Nanaimo. I had stayed behind to attend to the household duties while Felicity was away with her new lover. When he returned from Nanaimo he had with him a new briefcase, which he told me, contained some valuables. He asked if I would mind placing it under lock and key in my house safe.

"There was some inconsequence on that occasion but I didn't say a word to him about it. I just waited to see which direction this was all taking. I even have reservations about our present fishing trip to the Queen Charlotte Islands to meet with some new clients from New York. He told me that most are small business people. Why would he go to such an expense for so little in return? I've often wondered that.

"My dear Hanna, I must be boring you silly telling you these unimportant worries that I have."

"Not at all," Hanna answered. "I find it rather interesting. It could make good material for a soap opera."

"The last of my concerns that I will mention today," Penelope went on, "has to do with what I would call surveillance. On many occasions when I went to his place of business I thought I had seen a car following me. Sometimes I saw the same car parked on Military Street not far from the boarding house, always with two men in it. They looked like policemen to me but they could have been private detectives.

"When you called about your camera a few weeks ago, I made up my mind then to have a private talk with you. I felt that you might be the one person who could understand my concern in this relationship. I hope I wasn't wrong in my supposition. You see Hanna, there's also something about you that I can't put my finger on. Nothing bad, mind you, but I have a funny feeling. Don't be offended," she went on. "My world travels as well as my dealings with a partner who was an investigative reporter, shall I say, educated me in the art of 'being aware' of my surroundings. I may not look as if I have street smarts but believe me for certain things, I do. Sometimes it scares me to find out I should have avoided a certain person or place and I didn't. After that diatribe, all I really want to know from you is whether or not I should continue my relationship with Richard Taylor. Would you be kind enough to tell me the truth the way you see it!"

"Dear Penelope, you don't know what a relief this is to me," Hanna said. "From the first time I met you in your driveway with my little old Cadillac, I had the feeling that you and I were going to be friends. There are many things I want to tell you but you'll have to be patient with me. I can understand your uneasiness about your relationship with a man you don't know plus can't seem to get to know, for whatever reasons. When a woman is not comfortable in a personal relationship, she becomes edgy. She reacts to things instead of flowing with what is going on. It's almost like thinking that your partner or husband is cheating on you.

"What I'm going to tell you is probably going to shock the living life out of you. You may also be very angry with me, but trust me for now. What I did I had to do, otherwise it would not have worked out. And you, my dear friend, could possibly have been murdered! I can see your eyes getting bigger with a lot of questions popping up in your mind. They'll all be answered, I assure you. Just give me the time to go through my explanations and you'll fully understand everything. At least, I think you will."

Hanna began her story by telling Penelope that her real name was not Hanna Mueller but Joan Brent. That the house they were in was hers, inherited from her late father who had been a very successful heart specialist who passed away ten years ago. After graduating from UCLA in criminology, she joined the FBI fourteen years ago. From the very beginning with the Bureau, she was attached to special international investigations including smuggling of narcotics from all over the world. That meant she had to follow the trail of different individuals who were either the kingpin in an operation or in some way at a higher echelon. These smugglers were importing illegal drugs into the US, because of its proximity or because it was the preferred route, into Canada as well. Her trips to Victoria had been for that very purpose: "To find out as much as I could about Benjamin Malouf, also known as Richard Taylor."

The bomb had finally dropped. Penelope was absolutely horrified she wanted to ask all kinds of questions.

"What I'm going to say next, Penelope, is even more shocking, even very scary. You must be patient with me whilst I continue."

Joan (Hanna) went to the corner of the room, picked-up a briefcase and brought it back to the table. She first took a folder out and placed it on the table for future reference. As she handed Penelope a sheet of paper, she told her that Malouf was born in Lebanon of an Irish/Spanish/French mother and Lebanese father. His father had been the biggest smuggler, racketeer as well as all around gangster in the Middle East. He was trained in the art of terrorism. The father was especially good at training others, including his son. Malouf senior was killed some years ago in a shoot-out with police in Italy near the French border.

"Benjamin Malouf, as he is known, is a very well-educated man who has a master's degree in business administration from Harvard, along with a law degree from Oxford.

"He has also studied French literature in Paris. The man speaks five foreign languages fluently and flawlessly, which are; French, English, Spanish, Italian as well as German. As a youngster he was well trained in terrorism. His father was one of the best in that field. He made sure his knowledge would be passed on to his son. Malouf or Taylor, is also associated with one Italian crime syndicate in both Canada and the USA. His direct association is with the Vito and Vitriolli families in Montreal. He also has contacts with the Arminto family in New York City. These families control illegal gambling, prostitution, drug distribution, illegal weapons – you name it they do it, throughout North America. The families are also related by marriage. Their contacts with international suppliers of cocaine and heroin are through Benjamin Malouf. The drugs alone accounts for hundreds of millions of dollars to these families tax-free. The power that they wield because of their access to unlimited funds is mind-boggling. They would not hesitate one second to eliminate anyone who would dare get in their way.

"The proof of all this is in these next papers that I'm going to show you, there are some rather gruesome photographs. You may not want to look at all of them. They're really sickening but this is what these people do for a living. The FBI and the RCMP had planted several informers. They have disappeared never to be seen again. They've killed ordinary people, they've killed lawyers, and they've killed law enforcement officers. The list goes on and on."

As Penelope was looking at the papers Joan had given her with photographs attached to them, she could hardly believe what she was seeing. Her hands started to shake a bit. It was obvious to Joan that she was gradually realizing the full horror of the situation.

"Let's have a bit more wine before I continue," Joan said. "Since I started to tell you this incredible story, before we go much further with it, I'll jump to its conclusion so that you will not have to fear for yourself. You don't know how happy I am to have you here with me instead of worrying about you being on that boat. As law enforcement people, we believe this man to be one of the most dangerous criminals in the world. Benjamin Malouf AKA Richard Taylor is that man. I'm not going to give you every detail on what's going on at this very moment but just to reassure you, Malouf is being watched closely. A Coast Guard vessel is following him with experienced RCMP narcotics agents on board. Furthermore, in Victoria, his room was searched discreetly in addition to his warehouse being searched with a fine tooth comb as we speak."

Penelope could not believe her ears, she just kept shaking her head from side to side as if she didn't want to either hear anymore or believe anything she had just been told. She took a long sip of wine as if very thirsty. Joan refilled her glass immediately.

"I know it's hard for you to absorb all that I've told you but I want you to know that everything is OK back in Victoria. As a matter of fact I'm going to get the telephone for you to call your brother Sam. That might make you both feel a bit more comfortable."

***

When Sam answered the telephone he immediately realized it was his sister calling. He seemed to become very nervous and excited at the same time.

"Where are you, Sis?" he said. "Some things have happened here that are very upsetting, but anyway only Felicity and I know about it." He went on to tell Penelope that the RCMP had been to the house to search Richard Taylor's room. They then had gone to his warehouse since they had not found anything in the room except a book of telephone numbers they had taken with them.

Penelope told him not to worry, that she was in Los Angeles safe and in good hands. She asked him if he was sure that no one else knew the police had been to the house.

"No one else knows," Sam said, "only two officers came here, one was a male the other a female. You can be sure that we won't tell anyone either. When are you coming back?"

"I'll let you know Sam," Penelope replied, "but for the moment I'm going to stay here for a few more days. Make sure that Felicity does not tell anyone. Please Sam this is very important to all of us. Let's make sure the regular boarders don't find out right away. They'll eventually read about it in the newspaper, I'm afraid."

***

Prior to lunch, Joan had spoken with Bureau Chief Gerald Smudgely who informed her about the developments that had been reported from Ottawa as well as Victoria. Inspector Woodchuck had been advised to make direct contacts to save valuable time. She had also been told that the search of the warehouse had been very successful. So far, approximately eight hundred kilos of cocaine had been found, well-packaged, hidden in different items of plaster or furniture but the search was not over yet. It would be several hours

before every inch of that warehouse was account-
ed for!

"Have you had enough for today or do
you want me to continue as far as I can go with
this?" Joan asked.

"Please, Hanna – sorry, I mean Joan,
please continue" Penelope responded. "I'm so
glad I didn't commit myself fully to that relationship. I feel like a fool for not having been more
perceptive. The indicators were all there, I just
couldn't put them together. Because I had no one
to confide with, it was hard for me to see what was
going on. I'm so furious right now. How could I
not have seen this," she concluded.

"Before I go on with this dreadful story I
want you to know that my superior and all the police agencies involved are aware that you were
being used. Remember the Sunday we were on the
boat-ride together? I truly wanted to tell you to be
careful, but I couldn't. It would possibly have
damaged an international investigation that had
been ongoing for more than three years. Whilst I
was trying to figure out a way to tell you about
this, Malouf was always around. I was afraid that
if you said anything to him about drugs it would
make him suspicious.

"I'm not convinced that you should fly to
meet with him on the fishing trip, but if you don't
he'll really get suspicious. It's up to you, Penelope.
We can only offer you protection once the boat
docks at the final destination either Port Edward
or Prince Rupert. Unknown to Malouf, Captain

McMillan is acting as an undercover RCMP officer and he's fully aware of your situation.

"I think that you've heard enough for today, so let's go to Palm Springs for an overnight
stay. I have some friends there who will put us up.
Good food and wine are probably the best remedy
before you fly back tomorrow. Don't you think so
Penelope?"

CHAPTER EIGHTEEN…

Sergeant Popleski had been informed by private radio channel that the search of Taylor's Import/Export warehouse on the Gorge Waterway in Victoria had been successful. Over eight hundred kilos of cocaine had been found along with valuable information concerning bank accounts, names, telephone numbers etc. He was also told the search was not finished as yet!

Inspector Woodchuck had told Popleski to be careful. The law enforcement people were all aware as to the identity of the other "fishermen" they were going to encounter in the Queen Charlottes. The Inspector was sure the uncles would be well protected by Gabby and his henchmen. The Inspector asked Popleski to keep a special lookout for Penelope Woodspring and old Tom McMillan, who was putting his life in danger by being alone with Malouf. He further informed the Sergeant that he, a couple of constables, along with Smudgely of the FBI with possibly two or three of his agents, were flying into Prince Rupert on a special charter to lend a hand at the appropriate time. Woodchuck would inform Popleski where they were all going to be by late afternoon tomorrow, or possibly early the following day.

Taylor was in a cheerful mood and appeared to be quite pleased with Captain McMillan's navigation skills. He told the captain they had to make a stop in Winter Harbor close to the northern tip of Vancouver Island, to pick up Miss Woodspring who was flying in to come along on the fishing trip. Did the captain know where it was?

"I certainly do, sir," said McMillan. "My former brother in-law lives there. How long will we be stopping as perhaps I could pay him a quick visit? You see my sister died three years ago; the poor man never got over it. We'll reach Winter Harbor in about ninety minutes and still have some daylight left."

"Yes you certainly can visit your brother in-law. I was planning to stop over night, then proceed to Bella Bella tomorrow morning. Do you think that this is feasible, Captain?"

"It certainly is, Mr. Taylor. After we leave Winter Harbor, we can go around the northern tip of Vancouver Island head towards FitzHugh Sound and follow the Ferry Passage right up to Bella Bella. Here, let me show you on this map where our final destination is. There's Port Edward, we can stay in the Inside Passage, follow the Ferry route all the way. By doing that we'll avoid any stormy weather coming down from Alaska. Those cold winds can be treacherous at times. They bring on swells of fifteen to twenty five feet high though I know that this boat of yours can handle them. She was made for rough weather; she can take it with the best of them. The Giddley

Boat Company of Penetanguishene Ontario built
this boat. I happen to know the little Englishman
who designed it, Lloyd was his name. He used to
design fast-moving mine sweepers called corvettes
for the Canadian Navy during the war.

"His technique is unique in North America. You're very fortunate to have a boat designed
as well as built by that man. We can keep pace
with the best on the ocean plus pass them easily as
long as we have enough fuel. Bella Bella will be a
good place for refueling."

Richard was very pleased to have hired
this man who knew his seamanship and obviously
had a good knowledge of boat construction. The
five thousand dollars he had given him for this trip
was well spent. When they arrive in Port Edward,
Richard had told McMillan that he would be there
for a day or two.

Taylor had not planned any fishing until
the expected meeting with the other 'family'
members.

Knowing this, old Tom had told him if he
didn't mind, he would go visit one of his sisters
who lived in Prince Rupert, as he had not seen her
in over a year. "You see, Mr. Taylor, being born
to a large family in British Columbia gives one
'visiting rights' all over the province."

That, Richard thought, *would be the perfect time to meet with the uncles and exchange
gifts.* He wouldn't have to be concerned about
McMillan being present, thus any potential problems. He couldn't believe his luck since arriving
in Victoria, it seemed all possible problems were

being taken care of quite smoothly. Still his experience warned him to be careful with people he did not fully trust. What to do with Penelope was the problem to solve.

***

Most of the younger members of the crime syndicate would not have known who Tom McMillan really was. The West Coast had not been infiltrated by any organized criminal elements until about three to four years ago. Tom had been retired from the police force for ten years, his cover was perfect. Besides, he was such a good actor.

After docking in Winter Harbor, Tom left to pay a visit to his 'brother in-law.' What Taylor didn't know was that Tom had an old friend, also retired from the RCMP, who had moved to this quiet community. From his friend's home he would place a call to Inspector Woodchuck in Victoria to up-date him on the 'fishing' situation.

After greeting his old friend, Tom asked him if he could use the telephone for a very important call. Because he could trust his friend, he told him to sit still and listen to the conversation. McMillan informed the Inspector about the new developments of the trip, including Penelope's arrival, their destination as well as the navigation route they were going to follow. The Captain said that once docking was completed in Port Edward, he would be traveling to Prince Rupert in a rented car to visit his sister. He would wait there for the next instructions from Woodchuck. Tom mentioned that Taylor had said he would not require his services for at least forty-eight hours after they arrived in Port Edward. He was going to visit some friends and their guests on some other fishing boat already waiting there for him. He wondered what if anything he should do about Miss Woodspring's presence

The Inspector thanked McMillan. He told him to stay with his sister in Prince Rupert until he heard from Woodchuck that the "coast" was clear, again warning him to be extremely cautious until he reached his destination. "Keep an eye for Penelope," said the Inspector.

Tom thanked his old friend, had a couple of beers with him, talked about old times and on his request decided to spend the night instead of returning to the boat.

***

The next morning Tom returned to the boat early where Taylor and Penelope, who had arrived by seaplane, were waiting and ready to set off on the final leg of the trip.

Captain McMillan started the engines. They were on their way to the North Island, FitzHugh Sound, and Bella Bella. When they started moving towards the open sea, Taylor inquired about the traveling time to reach Bella Bella.

"It all depends on the weather," Tom said. "We could be there within a couple of hours. The scenery between here and there is just awesome," added the captain.

During that time Penelope had gone back to the cabin section. She thought for a moment that she should have put her anger aside and that coming along on the boat might just be somewhat dangerous for her. Of course she was mad, mad at herself for not seeing Taylor for what he was. She had to hide her feelings in fear of suffering a worst fate at the hands of an unscrupulous, self-centered individual and most of all dangerous gangster. She thought of a scheme to get away from him once they docked wherever that was going to be. She hoped that she would be able to watch him get arrested along with his other friends. Fear was beginning to overtake her and she would have to gather up all her strength to keep her front until final destination. She remembered some of the dangerous trips she had taken with Jason McKee and survived to tell about them. Those thoughts gave her strength.

While she was sitting there alone she noticed that some screws from the wall paneling appeared to be lose. In taking a closer look she realized that this could be the place where Malouf had hidden the drugs. *Enough of this kind of thinking for now,* she thought and walked back to the deck.

***

Sergeant Popleski was trying to understand a message coming in on the special radio channel. It was from the Inspector in Victoria. Popleski asked the pilot to cut the engine pitch so that everyone could hear what was being said. They had lost track of Taylor and were just nearing Winter Harbor when the message came in.

After receiving the information regarding Taylor's route, together with instructions from Woodchuck, they proceeded to Winter Harbor to refuel before the long journey to Port Edward. By so doing, they didn't have to worry about being spotted by or losing their prey. After all they just wanted to get to their destination as well as prepare properly for a showdown!

The pilot told Popleski he could navigate this area with his eyes closed. He said that he would prefer to stay on the outside of FitzHugh Sound and access the Inside Passage at the base of Higgins Pass. "That way," he went on, "we could travel at full speed without hindrance. The ocean may be a bit rough, but the faster speed will be worth it." Popleski had no problem with the suggestion agreeing to go that route.

"The sooner we get there, the more time we'll have to prepare. I prefer to wait instead of having to rush, as fewer mistakes are made that way. Let's refuel, have a bite to eat and be on our way," said the happy leader.

***

Meanwhile in Los Angeles, Bureau Chief Gerald Smudgely called six of his agents to inform them to prepare for a trip to Canada. "We're going to northern British Columbia to a lumber town called Prince Rupert."

These men were aware of the investigation that had been ongoing for almost three years.

All were eager to put an end to the activities of this organized crime family.

The agents were informed of the latest details received from the Inspector in charge of operation 'Oceanside' in Victoria. The FBI had leased a modified DC-3 Cargo plane to transport their crew and equipment (firearms) to Victoria, there take on six RCMP constables with their equipment, and fly to Prince Rupert together. As this was on Canadian territory, Inspector Woodchuck was the officer in charge of the group. When the American group of agents arrived in Victoria, they were taken to RCMP headquarters to meet their counterparts with whom they would be working.

After a good dinner the whole group was taken to a large boardroom where Inspector Woodchuck gave them instructions as to exactly where they were going and what he thought was going to happen. The group looked like a fisherman's convention with their fishing gear. Once they reached their destination, small vans would be made available. They would separate into three different groups so as not to attract too much attention. The Inspector reminded the men they were dealing with very dangerous criminals who would not hesitate to kill them. "No one is to take extra chances," he emphasized.

"We know that on Malouf's boat we have three targets. The captain of the boat, who happens to be a retired RCMP Inspector, will not be there so we don't need to be concerned for his safety. There's a woman whom we have to rescue away from Malouf. She has no involvement in his drug business. She's being used as a cover by Malouf, our third target. Once we've identified our targets we'll make our move. We have photographs of who is supposed to be there but let's not forget the unknown factor. I'm sure these notorious criminals have brought some protection along with them. We need to be alert. Any questions gentlemen?"

"Yes Sir," said a young constable, "didn't you have a Coast Guard vessel disguised as a fishing boat with four men aboard follow Malouf from Victoria?"

"Thank you, I was just coming to that. Sergeant Popleski along with two constables plus the pilot of the vessel will be close by. As a matter of fact they were to get there ahead of Malouf and wait for my instructions. You'll recognize their boat by the three flags on the mast; at the very top is the American Flag followed by the Union Jack and the French flag.

"Bureau Chief Smudgely has informed us that a few days ago, a sixty-foot hacht had left Seattle on its way to Juneau, Alaska, for a pleasure trip. This vessel is registered to a numbered company out of Montreal, Quebec and would you believe, by pure coincidence, to a company owned by Vincent Vitriolli's family? In Seattle they were welcoming aboard the American 'Godfather' Leonardo Arminto along with his entourage. Gentlemen, I have a feeling that the crops are ready to be harvested! When we've attained a successful completion to operation 'Oceanside', it will be the biggest catch of contraband as well as the largest number of criminal 'executives' caught in this decade. You can all see the importance of being 100% alert. We can't afford the tiniest mistake to happen. I'm going to divide you in three groups of four; two Americans and two Canadians per group. That way, every team will know who's who.

"Any questions? Is everyone comfortable with the information? Good! Tomorrow morning at six we fly to Prince Rupert. Have a good night's rest; the next 48 hours are going to be exciting."

***

Captain McMillan informed Taylor they would reach the docks in Port Edward in about forty-five minutes. Richard went back to the cabin where Penelope was lying down, somewhat under the weather. In a way Richard was pleased that it happened, it kept her from asking too many questions during the voyage. She told him that once they reached port she had decided to take a taxi to the nearest airport and fly home.

He said that he was disappointed but did not insist on her staying for the return trip, thinking all the time that this saved him the trouble of dealing with her.

Richard was looking forward to meeting the old uncles whom he had seen a long time ago in Lebanon when his father was still alive. These men had succeeded in staying alive as well as out of prison all their lives, never caught doing anything that the law considered illegal. Even during the years of Prohibition when Leonardo was a young man running booze from the West Coast to the East Coast, his luck had held out. Richard (Benjamin) admired these old Mafioso for their courage and strong control of a large widespread family during a most difficult economic period.

He knew that Gabby would be there with the rest of them since there had not been a family gathering like this in a very long time. He started to wonder if there might not be some 'happenings' going on about him. It could very well be, since Gabby now knew the operation inside out. *No*, he thought, *I must push those thoughts away. In any case I'll have a real surprise for them if that's what they're thinking of doing.*

What no one knew except Benjamin, was that he had wired his vessel from bow to stern. He had placed a large amount of explosives ready to be detonated by remote control when required. His former experience in terrorism had been handy in setting up that little surprise, should it be needed. So, he decided that once they docked in Port Edward he would make sure he could activate his "set-up" in a matter of seconds, just in case!

Eight hundred kilos of cocaine hidden in the bowels of his boat, along with twelve million dollars in cash was certainly a big responsibility. He was sure Gabby didn't want to lose either of those two.

***

Woodchuck and his group had placed themselves in strategic areas around the harbor in Port Edward. They had seen the magnificent sixty-foot yacht moored at the west end of the docking area. Not far from it, Sergeant Popleski with his men were cleaning some fish they had caught. So far, the total law enforcement personnel around the waterfront was at twenty-five with enough firepower to start a small war. There wasn't very much action on the sixty-footer except for the two uncles who were walking around the outside deck. Gabby Vito was sunning himself enjoying a drink, totally unaware of the surveillance surrounding them.

***

At about eleven-thirty that Thursday morning they saw Malouf's craft approach the channel, just about ten to fifteen minutes away from docking. Everyone was put on alert; the climax of this investigation was about to be reached. The Inspector knew he had to wait until some sign of recognition in addition to the movement of packages occurring before they could storm the yacht. Tom McMillan had squeezed his vessel just in front of the big one as a smaller craft was leaving.

Very convenient for the transfer of drugs, thought the Inspector as he was watching through his binoculars. He also saw McMillan leave with Miss Woodspring and wave as they walked towards the village to a sign that indicated 'Car Rentals'.

Now, thought the Inspector, *this will save us a dangerous rescue procedure.* Everything was in place for the cat and mouse game to begin. How long it would go on depended on how soon they were going to move the drugs from Malouf's boat to the big yacht. They saw Malouf leave empty-handed and proceed toward the yacht. He was greeted with hugs on the deck. Within a few minutes they all disappeared inside the cabin.

Popleski and his crew had two other small vessels between them and Malouf's boat. He would not take a chance on moving anywhere since this would attract the attention of the men who were standing guard around the deck of the yacht. Patience was the key at this point. They were ready to move on a moment's notice as pre-arranged with the Inspector.

Lunchtime went by, mid-afternoon came, still no evidence of movement of any drugs from Malouf's boat. Since daylight lasts until approximately nine-thirty in the evening at this time of the year at that latitude, the wait could go on forever it seemed. Fortunately the weather forecast had been for clear skies and a full moon.

At about eight in the evening they saw Malouf leave the yacht to return to his own cruiser. Everyone was keeping a close eye on anything moving towards Malouf's boat. He went inside his cabin. After twenty high tension minutes Malouf came back out on deck, waved at one of the men on the yacht, signaling for someone to come over.

What happened next was almost unbelievable for these officers to see. Six men walked down the gangway of the sixty-footer, each carrying what appeared to be some kind of large canvas bag. It was hard to tell since these bags were folded. They were khaki in color and looked as though they could have been purchased from any army surplus store in any large city.

The men walked on Malouf's boat and one by one disappeared inside the cabin. Within fifteen minutes the first two men came back on deck, got off the cruiser carrying heavily stuffed Kit bags. They waited on the dock for the other men to show up before walking back to the yacht. The Inspector put everyone on alert and waited until the other four individuals as well as Malouf came off the boat walking in the direction of the bigger vessel carrying the kitbags.

Suddenly the dock area was illuminated with floodlights and twenty heavily-armed officers appeared out of nowhere. Fourteen of them went up the yacht's gangway and the other six surrounded Malouf and the carriers. In a matter of seconds they had control of both vessels obviously catching everyone by surprise.

Within a few moments they had the key figures in handcuffs. Gabby Vito was stunned and could not believe this was happening in the presence of his uncles who had led a charmed life all these years. On the dock, the RCMP officers had no trouble with the six men. Two of the constables had made sure to grab Malouf simultaneously as he was considered the most dangerous man around. On searching him they found a detonator of some kind in his pockets and carefully retrieved it. They immediately marched him to the vans that had arrived. The Kit bags were gathered together and the rest of the merchandise along with what appeared to be a very large amount of cash was seized. Meanwhile the rest of the crew from the yacht was taken away. The Sergeant informed the Inspector that there was a major problem on Malouf's boat as he had found a set of wires (leading to some explosives) in the open panels left exposed by Malouf since he didn't have time to close them before his arrest. An evacuation order was immediately given and a call was placed to get an explosive expert from the Armed Forces flown in at once. The whole area was cordoned off. The Coast Guard Patrol was put on alert to stop all incoming vessels to the area. Knowing the terrorist background of Malouf, the Inspector didn't want to take the risk of having any of his men hurt or killed. They had been lucky in securing the detonator from Malouf's pockets.

Soon after the action had stopped, the local news people had heard rumors of a big seizure of narcotics along with the arrest of some prominent crime figures from Canada as well as the States. Journalists were trying to get to the dock area to get pictures and statements. Officers who told them of the risk of a possible explosion stopped them. For further comments they were referred to Inspector Woodchuck the man in charge of operation 'Oceanside.' The Inspector realized that he must give them some bits of information to satisfy their curiosity and willingly did so. He told the press that as this operation was taking place on the Northern Coast of BC, at the same time in Montreal, Toronto, Vancouver, Seattle and New York, other individuals who were known to be part of these families were being rounded up.

"Operation 'Oceanside' is international in extent and as you can see, has been a great success. For the first time in two decades we have arrested the top echelon of organized crime in North America. I'll give you more details after we take care of the very dangerous explosive situation we have on hand. An Army bomb disposal expert has been called in and should be here within the next two to three hours. Once the problem is resolved we will give you access to the docking area and possibly the vessels involved.

"We do have some stock photographs for you, with information as to who these people are. Without the indispensible help of Bureau Chief Gerald Smudgely of the FBI Los Angeles office, we couldn't have achieved our objective as successfully as we have. This is a great international co-operation that also includes Interpol in South America. We'll have a press release for you in the morning with more details as to the quantities of drugs that were seized here and elsewhere."

Inspector Woodchuck made sure that Bureau Chief Gerald Smudgely stood close to him for the all important news photos.

***

When Penelope arrived in Victoria. she had a closed meeting with Sam and Felicity. She recounted how afraid she had been but was so mad and upset at Malouf for using her the way he had that her anger gave her the strength to carry her through. Because they wanted to know more she told them how she had convinced "Richard" she was not feeling well and was going to fly home from Prince Rupert. Penelope said she was a bit surprised that he didn't make a fuss at her leaving but didn't question it further. She even said that he looked relieved. She left the boat with Captain McMillan who rented a car and took her to the airport. At that moment of her story telling she suddenly realized the dangerous situation she had been in and started to cry.

The following morning the newspapers were full of photos of Taylor's Import/Export warehouse and the headlines read: **LARGEST DRUG BUST EVER... DRUG KINGPIN WORKING OUT OF VICTORIA!**

Then the story went on to say just how Benjamin Malouf, alias Richard Taylor had set up a business in Victoria which happened to be a front for organized crime and their drug distribution. The news people wanted to do interviews with the owner of the boarding house but she refused. Sam was sensible enough to let them know that he and his sister had nothing to do with these criminals but were victims of the biggest con-man in Canada. Any other information they would have to get from the Inspector in charge at the RCMP Headquarters in Victoria.

Penelope decided that it would be better if she went away to Hawaii for a week or two while this whole story died down. Sam took her to the airport telling her not to worry; he and Felicity would look after the boarding house at 13 Military Street.

~*~*~*~

www.ingramcontent.com/pod-product-compliance
Lightning Source LLC
Chambersburg PA
CBHW070103030726
47506CB00002B/580